THE LOST TYCOON

Book Five in the Baby for the Billionaire Series

by Melody Anne

COPYRIGHT

Printed and published in the United States of America.

Published by Gossamer Publishing Company

Editing by Nicole and Alison

DEDICATION

This is dedicated to a new and dear friend, Kathiey. I could sit and talk to her until all hours of the night. Wait! We do that already! I am so glad to know you, Kathiey, and I can't wait for the fun adventures ahead.

NOTE FROM THE AUTHOR

I CAN'T BELIEVE it is time for another book to come out! When you have a job that you love so much, it's never work — it's pure joy. This story begins so much differently than my other books do, and then it takes a few twists and turns that I wasn't expecting. That's what I love about writing. Nothing is set in stone. I can go where the story leads me, and I often do!

I am so excited about the new year. It promises many new adventures, and many new surprises for all of you. Thank you, as always, for the wonderful support you give me. I hope you enjoy my book about Bryson and Misty. I don't normally have favorite characters, but I have to say that I wept a few times with Misty. When I'm writing a story, I always talk to people I know about it; I listen to their opinions and accounts of relevant incidents in their lives. I'm deeply saddened to know that there are people out there like Misty; even worse, most of them don't get to experience a happy ending.

Thank you again for sticking with me. To win prizes each month, make sure you join me on Facebook, Twitter and my website. It's one of our ways of showing appreciation to all that you do for me.

A lot of love goes to my family and friends. I can't do any of this without you! I love you all! Now that the book is done, I'll come out of my cave and we'll have a pizza party!!

Melody Anne

A NOTE TO THE READER

I F YOU'VE READ the standard disclaimer, you'll know that this is a work of fiction. In fact, it's a work of romantic fiction, and as such it has just a bit of fantasy in it. We all want our drama and our happy endings, and to achieve that, I've taken liberties with certain procedures of the FBI, federal prosecution, and the United States Federal Witness Protection Program. It seemed only right.

BOOKS BY MELODY ANNE

BILLIONAIRE BACHELORS
*The Billionaire Wins the Game
*The Billionaire's Dance
*The Billionaire Falls
*The Billionaire's Marriage Proposal
*Blackmailing the Billionaire
*Runaway Heiress
*The Billionaire's Final Stand
*Unexpected Treasure
*Hidden Treasure – **Coming Soon**

BABY FOR THE BILLIONAIRE
+The Tycoon's Revenge
+The Tycoon's Vacation
+The Tycoon's Proposal
+The Tycoon's Secret
+The Lost Tycoon

RISE OF THE DARK ANGEL

-Midnight Fire – Rise of the Dark Angel – Book One

-Midnight Moon – Rise of the Dark Angel – Book Two

-Midnight Storm – Rise of the Dark Angel – Book Three

-Midnight Eclipse – Rise of the Dark Angel – Book Four –

Coming Soon

Surrender

=Surrender – Book One

=Submit – Book Two

=Seduced – Book Three

=Scorched – Book Four

CHAPTER ONE

I SWEAR I didn't see anything."

Her heartbeat thrashed in her ears as Misty Elton backed away.

"What in the hell were you snooping around for?" His eyes bulged and his fists balled tightly together.

"I was just looking for a sweatshirt because the apartment was cold. I swear. I didn't see anything." Misty was almost sobbing. Her eyes darted toward the door, and she inched toward it, away from his deadly fists, trying to lock her shaking knees together in her flight-or-fight response to what she saw in his face.

Hatred. Loathing. The very devil resided inside him — she was sure of it.

She had no doubt about the way this was going to end. When his voice rose like that, to an almost squealing pitch, when the corners of his mouth tightened and when his fingers firmed, turning his hands into brutal, merciless weapons, it meant she was going to get hurt.

The evidence stood out, practically glowing like a neon light. She'd never before had such a great wish to turn back the clock, to undo one mistake. She'd only been searching for a sweatshirt in the trunk in the room — that was all — and instead she'd found his stash. And that was the moment he'd found her. If he'd come in only a minute later, she'd have closed the lid and rushed from the room, and he never would have known.

As he took a step closer, her stomach turned over. This was worse than usual — this wouldn't be a typical punishment. She knew his intentions from the cold fury of his gaze.

"I promise I won't slip up, won't tell another soul what I saw," she pleaded. "I swear. It was only a sweatshirt I was looking for!"

"Come here, Misty!" he growled, ignoring her plea as she took another step back. "Now!"

In the past, such words from him stopped any trace of resistance. She knew that if she ran, it could only end one way: he'd pursue her and give her at least one broken bone. If she screamed or cowered, she'd see his eyes light with pleasure as he continued to pummel her.

She'd been with this man for a whole year. In the beginning, she'd thought he was so impressive, a good-looking cop who wanted her. *He'd actually wanted her!* It hadn't taken long for her to see his true colors, but from the moment he'd set his sights on her, it was too late.

Once Jesse wanted something, he either got it or that something disappeared forever. She'd discovered that the hard way — the painful way. She was trapped. No one and nowhere to turn to. Her only escape from him ever was when she worked part time at a local diner, and even then, he would show up at random intervals to check in on her. If he saw the smallest indication of flirting — and just talking to another man usually counted as flirting to him — Misty would feel Jesse's fists when she got home.

The one time she'd tried to leave him... A shudder passed through her. She didn't have time to think about that — she needed to stay focused on this moment, on this situation. If she lost concentration for even a second, he would pounce, and she knew that this time she wouldn't see daylight ever again.

He kept his eye on her as he sat on the edge of the bed and untied his work boots, looking as if he had all the time in the world. In his mind he did. Still, the faster he got out of his clothes, the more ready he would be to torture her in the most sadistic ways possible.

She thought about running while he was tugging first one boot off and then the other, but it wouldn't give her enough of a head start. No. She had to plan this just right.

Lately the beatings had been worse than ever before — bad enough, in fact, that she couldn't take it anymore, even if she died trying to escape. And she might. She'd saved some money — money he'd be furious about if he knew what she was doing — and she'd been planning on leaving in two days. That was when he had the long shift. She'd be several hundred miles away before he ever knew.

Even with his resources, he wouldn't find her — not this

time. She shuddered when she thought back to the last time she'd tried to leave. She was trying to concentrate on the here and now, but her mind had other ideas. That attempted escape had landed her in the hospital for two weeks in intensive care. She'd even tried pressing charges, but somehow the paperwork had been buried. He'd warned her that if she tried that again, she wouldn't wake up.

She believed him.

So now they were in a face-off. She was so close to freedom, so close...

"Are you listening to me, bitch?"

Misty froze. He'd stood back up and drawn a couple of steps closer to her.

"I swear, Jesse, I didn't see anything. I won't tell a soul. I was just looking for a sweatshirt."

"Yeah. That's what my last ex said, too. Then the whore ran to the cops — my buddies. They were good enough to tell me about the lying little tramp. Do you see her around, Misty?"

"No," she practically sobbed.

"Yeah, no one will see her around again," he said, with a glint in his eyes that increased her terror. "And no one will ever run to my buddies spilling lies about me again, either."

"I wouldn't do that," she said. What was the fastest escape? If she could get away, she'd be fine. But she couldn't let her eyes dart around, or he'd see it. And he was still in his police uniform, and she was very aware of the gun on his hip. What would he tell the cops, the brotherhood who would vouch for him?

Probably that she'd brought in the drugs, he'd seen them

and confronted her, and then she went crazy. She was sure he'd plant a gun on her, make it look convincing. They'd pat him on the back, tell him he was one lucky bastard to have gotten out alive.

She'd become nothing but some paperwork, her body cremated because there was no one to pay for a casket and bury her, and because he wouldn't want even her body to remain on this earth. She'd go up in smoke and never be thought of again.

Maybe that was for the best. Her life was one long nightmare. Wait! She was thinking of giving up? The hell she would. Everyone deserved a chance to survive — to really live. She was no different.

Her spine stiffened. There was no way she'd just roll over. This man might very well get away with killing her, and he might do it all too easily — it might be a short-lived battle — but at least she'd go down fighting.

"Stay here!" And Jesse had no doubt she'd do exactly that. Why would she try to escape? She'd tried that once and it had only made her punishment worse.

He moved toward his private room across the short hallway, and she heard *the* drawer open. Oh, shit! He was planning to handcuff her to the bar he had attached to the solid kitchen table he'd had specially reinforced for one purpose: to inflict unimaginable pain. He'd done this before. He'd ripped off her shirt and beat her — immobilized, with her arms and legs in shackles — until she was unconscious and bloody.

To this day, she couldn't look at her back in the mirror; she was too afraid to see the tangle of scars there. With her eyes filled with tears, she made a silent dash to the living room, grabbed her purse off the small table, and swung open the front door.

She ran down the hallway, fleeing toward the stairs of their apartment building as soundlessly as a fawn bouncing through a meadow. Her feet moved full speed ahead as if the hounds of hell were after her. At least one was — that was for sure.

She slipped into the stairwell, the fire door making a loud click behind her as she barreled down, making it two levels before she heard the fire door open again.

"Get back here now!"

She didn't take the time to lean over the railing and look up the winding staircase. She was still two flights ahead of him, but with three to go. The elevator was slow. If he turned back and took that, she'd make it out way ahead of him. But no such luck. She heard the door shut and she knew he was coming after her. At least he was barefoot. That would slow him down.

Almost flying, one hand barely on the banister to keep her from taking a headlong plunge, she made it to the bottom floor, pushed through the door, and then ran down the last hall to the wide front doors of the building. She thrust down the bar, yanked open the door, and rushed into the parking area. It was early morning, the light just beginning to displace the shadows of night, and there *would* be witnesses. He wouldn't care, though. Nothing would stop him if he got his hands on her.

Once she was scrambling through the huge parking lot, she didn't slow down as she pulled her car keys from her purse and looked up to see her car, a car he didn't know about. It seemed miles away. So far! Too far!

Time stood still and her lungs burned as she attempted her frantic escape.

"The longer you drag this out, Misty, the worse it's going to be for you."

Damn! He'd made it through the doors. How far ahead was she?

She knew she shouldn't, but she looked back. He was walking, thinking he had plenty of time, but he was too close still for her comfort. Thank goodness for the extra weight he'd put on, making it more difficult for him to run.

Her heart thundered in her chest, and she stumbled, but she caught herself at the last second before she crashed onto the broken asphalt.

If she fell, it would all be over. He'd drag her back upstairs by her hair. The neighbors wouldn't even bother calling the cops. They were all terrified of Jesse, and they all knew that any call would be thrown out anyway. Even if he did pound her to a pulp right there, people would turn their backs.

She'd received the pitying glances, the incredulous looks. People wondered why she stayed. She wanted to tell them it wasn't by choice — she wanted to beg for help. But she wouldn't involve anyone else. This was her misery and she would either be freed from this hell or she'd die trying.

Her sides had begun to ache, but the car was now close. She skidded to a stop a moment later, her key ready, her hand unbelievably steady as she pushed it into the lock on the first try. Wrenching open the door, she jumped into the driver's seat and immediately pressed the key to the ignition — this time not so lucky. She'd missed it.

"Please," she begged whoever might be listening, and this time when she pressed the key forward, thankfully, it slid into the ignition.

She turned the key so hard that she was afraid she'd break it, but her car started on the first try. The fates must be lining up in her favor.

"Get out of that car, Misty!"

So close.

He was so very close. She backed the car out of the parking spot and saw him only about ten yards behind her. *"Please, please, please..."* she begged as she threw the car into drive and slammed the gas pedal all the way to the floor.

As she pulled up to the exit from the lot, she glanced into the rearview mirror again, locking gazes with Jesse. A cold shiver of dread passed through her when she saw how near he was, almost to the bumper of her car. A look of murder was in his eyes, and it was clear what would happen if he got his hands on her. By the time he was done, she'd want to die.

There was no going back now. There was no need to. She had everything she needed in this little car, her escape a couple of days early, but well planned out.

Pulling onto the street, she sped away, breathing heavy as she traveled through Billings, Montana. If he called her car in... If he somehow caught up to her... If...

No. She wouldn't think that way. She'd gotten away. She would stay away. He didn't know which way she was going — he had no way of finding her. This was her car — it was a junker, a twenty-year-old Honda with more than two hundred thousand miles on the odometer, ripped upholstery and no working heater, but it was hers, debt free.

He couldn't report it stolen — he couldn't take it from her. He hadn't even known about it until just this moment, which had given her another advantage. He'd thought he'd be able to chase her down the street, wait for her to tire out. He hadn't been expecting her to drive off.

She just prayed it had been too dark for him to take down her license plate number. His eyes had been connected with hers in the mirror, she reminded herself. He hadn't been looking anywhere near her license plate.

"I'm free," she said aloud. Maybe she'd actually believe it if she repeated it enough.

When she reached the edge of town and jumped onto the freeway, she let out her first real sigh of relief. When she made it a hundred miles away, her white knuckles relaxed on the steering wheel.

Her body shaking, she didn't stop moving until she was in Washington State, where she pulled off the I90 at a truck stop in Spokane. She got out and pumped in some gas, letting the cool wind glide across her. Her nerves were still frazzled, but she was free. For now, anyway.

Inside the store, she found a few snacks that didn't cost too much and poured herself a large coffee to keep awake. She wasn't far enough away. She needed to keep going.

When she stepped back outside, a police cruiser circled by, and her eyes met the officer's. Terror seized her heart, but she knew it didn't show in her face. She was prepared for this, and she knew that cops looked for signs of guilt.

If she didn't give this one a reason to talk to her, he would pass on by. Walking with confidence, or what she hoped looked like confidence, she opened her car door casually and slid into the driver's seat, taking her time situating her food and drink and buckling her seat belt.

When the officer drove away, she allowed the breath that had been caught in her throat to rush out, and she sagged in her seat. As much as she kept telling herself she was fine, she wasn't. She wouldn't be until she made it to such a big city that Jesse would never find her again.

Misty stopped only one more time. A few hours later, she pulled into a rest stop, used the bathroom, picked up another cup of coffee, and then jumped back onto the freeway.

"Please give me a little bit longer," she begged her car, and the old thing must have listened, because just as the sun was starting to sink down in the sky, she entered Seattle — her new home. For a while.

This was a city she could get lost in; this was a place he wouldn't be able to find her — not when there were three and a half million people in the Seattle metropolitan area. It wasn't like Montana, where Billings was the largest city, with just over a hundred thousand people.

She wasn't thrilled at the idea of living in a big city, but she was excited to escape Jesse, excited to begin her life at the age of twenty-eight. It should have begun a very long time ago, but she wouldn't dwell on that — she would focus on the here and now.

She'd escaped.

After checking into a cheap motel, Misty got to work. She took the contents from the bag she'd had stored in her trunk and began her transformation. A couple of hours later, when she looked at herself in the mirror, she was almost unable to recognize the woman gazing back at her. Black hair hung straight down her back, makeup covered the bruises that would finally have time to heal before new wounds were inflicted, and contacts changed her green eyes to brown.

With a new name, she wouldn't be found. With a new life, she wouldn't be afraid. This was truly a new start.

CHAPTER TWO

"IT TOOK A long time to find you, Ms. Elton."

Oh, no. Oh, no. Misty looked up into the steady gray gaze of the giant of a man standing in front of her. No! She was safe. It had been a year. A full year. It was only a few months ago that she had let down her guard, had decided it was safe to live again, had gone back to her natural brown color.

Jesse had moved on, surely. He wouldn't have stayed single this long. He had to have a woman to boss around — to beat up on — by now. He would still hate her, still want her dead, but he wouldn't still be searching for her. There was just no possible way.

"I...uh...I don't know who you're referring to," she gasped, and she crept toward the door to the back room. She was working a crappy job at a fast-food joint. The place was nondescript, a bit seedy, in fact, and they hadn't blinked when she'd given them her false name, her poorly done fake ID. She sure as heck wouldn't eat the food there, not with their lax views on hygiene. They hadn't even made her get a food handlers card. But the job was working for her for now, allowing her to save up for her next move — though she wasn't saving much.

If she could just get through the door, get to her locker, then she'd be able to grab her Taser. She'd started leaving it in her purse just a few months ago. Up until that point, she'd carried it on her, keeping the small, but hopefully effective, device in her pocket, just in reach of her shaking fingers.

This was what happened when you grew careless. This would be what killed her.

"Please don't be afraid. I'm here to help you."

"I don't need help. You have the wrong person," she said, her voice more steady. He was watching her move toward the door, but he wasn't taking a menacing step toward her — wasn't reaching for the gun she knew he had to have on him.

She was close, so close. Inching a bit closer to the door, she kept her eyes on his hands. Those would tell her his next move. She'd become an expert at reading Jesse through his hands. The second they clenched she'd known she was in trouble.

This man's hands were sitting idly at his hips, just sort of hanging there. "Can I please sit down with you for a few minutes of your time? I won't ask you to go anywhere alone with me." His voice, she was sure, was supposed to convey trustworthiness.

That made her more suspicious.

"Sorry. I have to get something from the back room." She took her chances and darted through the door, not looking back as she made her way to her locker. Thankfully, it was open, since the only other person on shift was a nice kid whom she actually trusted. She quickly reached into her purse.

When her fingers curled around the small Taser, she felt her fear dwindle. The device wasn't deadly, but it would knock a large man down long enough for her to get away.

"Ms. Elton, please…"

He'd followed her. And he was grabbing her arm.

Misty didn't hesitate. She turned back to face him and pushed the button on her weapon. His eyes widened with shock —literally! —followed by a shot of pain as thousands of volts of electricity traveled through his skin into his stomach.

He released her arm, and Misty took a step toward the door, she was planning to get the hell away — far away from him and this place. It was time to find a new city. She'd stayed too long, far longer than she had originally planned, but her car had died, and she hadn't saved enough to move again yet. Almost but not quite. The heck with it now, though. She'd jump onto a bus and live in a shelter for a while.

She wouldn't be returned to Jesse. Never again.

When the man's hand snaked out and grabbed her leg, tripping her, Misty let out a gasp of dismay. She got ready to use the stun gun again, longer this time. *If at first you don't succeed…*

"I don't think so," he growled between clenched teeth. He smacked the gun from her hand and pinned her under his huge body.

"Let me go," she screamed, struggling beneath him.

"Give me a second," he moaned, not letting her up as he worked on catching his breath.

Yeah, that was going to happen. Sure, she was going to wait until he was back to full strength before she tried to escape.

"You won't get away with this." She was trying to sound more confident than she actually was. This was bringing back the nightmares of the way Jesse had tortured her. Her struggles against the stranger increased as she got a hand free and punched him in the face.

Her hand throbbed from the hit, but it didn't seem to faze him in the least.

"If you hadn't used a damn stun gun on me, we wouldn't be rolling around on this filthy floor. Who in the hell told you it was an effective weapon? The things only *stun* your attacker for a brief moment, and certainly not me. Not someone with training! Now hold on; my damn stomach is rolling."

"Yeah, right, I'll just wait for you to get all better, because I have a death wish!" She managed to lift her knee and slam it against his groin, though it wasn't a direct hit — his thigh took the brunt of the impact.

"Dammit!" Bryson yelled as his entire body stiffened.

No, he didn't release her. He wrenched her two hands above her head and held her legs down with one of his own as he breathed heavily against her neck.

"Am I interrupting?"

Bryson Winchester groaned again, this time in utter embarrassment, as he turned to see his partner standing in the doorway with a grin on his face.

"Can you give me a hand here?" Bryson growled.

"Yeah, that five-foot-nothing girl looks like a real handful," Axel said with a laugh.

"Who are you people?" Misty fired off. Their attitudes confused her. Jesse had never acted that way — almost offhand — when he was about to beat her. Deadly, yes, offhand, no. The man staring at the human pretzel that she and the giant were making on the floor looked amused, not deadly.

"I knew I should have brought some popcorn," the guy said, not even trying to hide his enjoyment at his partner's struggle.

"Would you shut the hell up and give me a hand, Axel?" Bryson snapped, then turned back to glare at her. "I was trying to tell you who I am before you did your best to inflict permanent damage on certain body parts." He was finally starting to catch his breath again, but just as the pain began to dwindle, he found he was starting to have another problem.

Oh, this was *so* not good. How in the hell could he even think of getting aroused? His groin was throbbing, his stomach still rolling from the Taser, and she was still fighting him.

There had to be something immensely wrong with him if he could get even the slightest bit turned on in this situation.

But he'd been so busy trying to defend himself from this shockingly strong woman that he was just now realizing that the two of them were lying flush against each other, and though she might be petite, she carried some killer curves. *Yeah, great self-defense, bozo!*

Bryson would absolutely *never* hear the end of this if he stood up with an erection. *Breathe!* he commanded himself. *Think of mom, grandma, the damn Yankees.* Yeah, that would deflate him.

"Help!" Misty screamed, and Bryson could now add a splitting headache to his list of injuries. Her voice could have shattered glass, and it was aimed right into his ear.

"That's it," he snapped, and he moved off her so quickly that she was stunned into immobility.

He didn't wait for round two. He jerked her body up and twisted her arms behind her back. He slapped a pair of handcuffs on her.

"See, you got it under control," Axel said. He was laughing again.

"I'll remember this," Bryson grumbled at his partner while leading the woman out of the back room.

"Stop! I'm calling the police," said a pimply-faced teenage boy who stood frozen in all his bravery by the front counter.

"Took you long enough to check on your co-worker, son," said Axel, his hazel eyes twinkling.

"I was cleaning the bathroom," the kid replied. Then he realized he was making excuses for himself to the men kidnapping his co-worker. He was obviously terrified, but Bryson had to give it to him — he wasn't backing down.

"Call the CIA," Misty shouted. There was no way she trusted the cops. She didn't know whether a person even could call the CIA, though.

"Uh, shouldn't I just call 911?" William asked as he wavered at the counter.

"No!" Misty cried.

That one word revealed more to Bryson than anything else she'd done — and in the span of about five minutes, she'd done plenty.

"I'll…uh…call the CIA," her co-worker said with doubt.

"It's OK, kid. We're the FBI," Bryson told him. He reached

into his jacket pocket and pulled out his badge.

"No, they aren't, Will," Misty broke in. "Those are fake badges."

The young man's head snapped over to her. "Okay." He'd only just turned eighteen, and he had no idea what to believe. Nothing like this was supposed to happen to him.

Axel spoke next. "Trust me, kid. We're the real deal." He also pulled out his badge, and, approaching Will cautiously, he handed him his card with the phone number of headquarters on it. "Look at it. And you can call this number to verify."

Will took the card and walked to the phone, keeping an eye on all three of them. Bryson had a difficult time not laughing. He'd humor the kid. He didn't want to admit it, but his groin area was still throbbing, and he was grateful to be able to just stand there a couple of extra minutes. The last thing he wanted to do was limp to the damn SUV.

Will dialed the number, and Bryson knew when the call was connected, because the kid's eyes bugged out. Yeah, that tended to happen the first time a person reached FBI headquarters. Bryson still remembered when all that had impressed him.

Axel grabbed Bryson's badge and shoved it over so the kid could ask whether both of them were agents. When Will was satisfied, he hung up the phone and faced them. "It's legit, Marcy," he said, his eyes shining with sudden hero worship.

At least he was using the fake name she'd come up with, one close enough to her own name that she wouldn't confuse herself.

But Misty knew she was sunk anyway. "Thanks for trying, Will," she said, more sad than anything else. This was the end.

They were now going to take her to their car and drive her out into the woods, and then her body would never be found. "I really liked working with you."

Bryson was confused by the change in her tone, but he didn't focus on it. He just started leading her outside after telling Axel to collect her belongings. The fight had left her, and she didn't wrestle against him as he moved to the vehicle and opened the back door.

"Watch your head," he warned her, and she slid inside.

When he climbed in with her, she looked straight ahead. One tear slid down her cheek, but other than that, not a sound or reaction.

"Now, Ms. Elton, can we speak?" he asked.

"Why not?" she said, her voice defeated.

"If I take off the handcuffs, do you promise not to attempt to hit me again?"

"What good would it do? The Taser didn't even faze you," she replied.

"Oh, it fazed me. I may not work properly for a while," he said, a mocking grin lighting up his face.

"I won't struggle anymore. Just get this done, please. I'm tired of being afraid, anyway."

"Good. We believe you are a witness to the activities of Jesse Marcus. We would like any information you can give us."

Yep. This was it. They wanted to see what she knew, whom she'd told, and whether there was anyone else they had to kill. And then they'd off her.

"I haven't told anyone anything," she said, a tiny but unquenched hope in her chest making her plead for her life, no matter how useless it was.

"I believe you, Ms. Elton. I promise you, I'm not working for Mr. Marcus. On the contrary. I'm going to make sure the bastard doesn't hurt anyone ever again."

Maybe it was his tone, maybe his words, but Misty slowly lifted her eyes and met his gaze. Questions stared back at him. He waited, looking at her without blinking, trying to convey to her that he was, indeed, the good guy.

"Who are you?" she finally whispered.

"I'm Special Agent Bryson Winchester, and this is my partner, Special Agent Axel Carlson. We're the men who are going to lock up the man you've been running from."

He didn't break the connection of their eyes, didn't move as she processed his words.

Then it was all over. Misty sagged against the back of the seat as she let herself go for the first time since she'd run from Jesse a year ago. She let go of the fear, let go of the pain, let go of it all, and cried.

She didn't know if she'd be able to stop — didn't know if this was it for her. She'd gone so far holding it all in, staying strong, and now that the dam had a crack in it, maybe she would just burst apart and be like that forever.

At some point, she found herself cradled against this stranger's chest, her tears soaking his once pristine shirt. She didn't even have the energy to care. She just let it all out, every single emotion she'd been bottling up for so long. He stopped talking, and just ran his hand through her hair.

Somewhere in the middle of all of this, the SUV began moving, but she didn't care. She couldn't care. She just kept on crying — out of relief, out of pain, out of hope.

CHAPTER THREE

BRYSON PACED RESTLESSLY through the suite as he waited for Misty to finish her shower. It seemed much easier to bring her back to the hotel, get her a room, and let her take some time to compose herself before they questioned her.

It had taken over an hour to convince her that they were really from the FBI and they were there to help her. Well, if he had to be completely honest, they were there to help their case. But, by getting Jesse behind bars, they were helping Misty.

That was important.

She had more information stored in her brain than she realized. Jesse Marcus was the true definition of a bad cop, and Bryson was going to bust his ass. The man was mixed up in drugs, prostitution, and murder. He was going down.

At first, Bryson had thought that Misty might be involved in it all, but after reviewing the surveillance tapes, checking into her tragic history, and basically learning everything he could about her, he knew she was innocent. Sometimes his radar was wrong, but he didn't think so in this case.

She'd simply been in the wrong place at the wrong time, and she was now paying a high price for crossing paths with that man. Misty Elton was lucky to be alive.

And Bryson intended to keep her that way.

"What do you want to eat?"

Bryson turned to find Axel leaning quietly against the door, a bored smirk on his face. This was a part of their job they both hated — babysitting.

"Is everything secure?" he asked, ignoring the question.

"Yep. We're all clear outside. I had a nice stroll," Axel said.

"Good. I want to keep the local law enforcement out of this. She doesn't trust them, and frankly, I understand why. We'll never get her to talk if the men in blue show up."

"Yeah, it's cases like these that make me appreciate my job more. I don't know how men like Jesse ever pass the tests to become police officers."

"We both know it happens," Bryson said with a sigh.

"Okay, I'm starved. What should I get?" Axel asked again.

"Burgers will be fine," Bryson said. He had no appetite at the moment.

"Nah. We had those the last few nights. Let's do Chinese."

"Why ask my opinion, Axel, when you're just going to get whatever you feel like?"

"'Cause it's always fun to annoy you." Axel grabbed his coat and headed from the room.

The two men had been colleagues for the past five years, had been through some less than ideal cases, and they knew each other well enough to keep alive. Axel was his best friend, his confidant, his brother-in-arms.

The shower clicked off and Bryson tensed. He didn't understand why this woman was getting under his skin. She was just another victim in a long line of them — just another case. There was no reason to take any of this personally. No reason to get worked up over it. It was a standard case, pretty much cut-and-dry. They get her testimony; they lock her slimy ex up.

A doubt nagged at him. What if she was too afraid to get up in the witness box? Well, his job was to give her confidence, make sure she knew she was protected. It wasn't an easy task, because they didn't know how many of the policemen Jesse was working with were corrupt.

He had no doubt that if Jesse got his hands on her again, he would kill her.

However, if she pulled out, they had quite a few other witnesses. It was just that they didn't want this case to fall apart for any reason, and if all the witnesses got jumpy and bailed, Jesse would walk. That was unacceptable.

He was really just worried about the case. That was all. So why this immediate need to take this woman's burdens upon himself? He'd held many women while they sobbed in his arms. And nothing. He'd never felt the slightest trace of emotion stirring inside himself.

Walking over to the patio door, frustrated, he flung it open, and a strong gust blew inside the room, flipping his tie over his shoulder and cooling the room instantly. Seattle was definitely a cold place in February. He'd rather be home in Montana, truth to tell — though the winters were harsher, rain wasn't as constant a presence there. First choice? His place in L.A. The women wore far less clothing, which was always a plus.

Especially since those women went for him in a big way. Bryson's deep tan never had a chance to fade, because he did a lot of work in warmer climates, and the bright gray eyes in his lean face and his solid jawline set him apart from other men. He wasn't someone easily ignored.

Bryson could certainly turn on the charm, and he knew when to use it to his advantage. The intense, almost animal light that would enter his eyes when he was interrogating a suspect had elicited more than one confession. His smile could either inspire confidence or inflict terror, depending on the mood he wished to set.

Though Bryson could be frightening as hell, he normally left the bad-cop routine to Axel. His colleague enjoyed it more than he did nowadays. Turning thirty-five last year had seemed to be a pivotal moment for him — he must be mellowing in his old age.

Sheesh. He wanted to kick himself. He was thinking like he already had one foot in the grave. What was the matter with him?

It had to be this city. Seattle was so damn gloomy, always messing with his mind. The sooner he could persuade Misty to hop on a plane with him, come home and give her deposition, the better off they would all be.

Yes, he could force her into testifying, subpoena her, keep her locked up, but he'd rather not put her through more trauma. She'd been abused enough. If he could get her to do this willingly, it would be so much better for them all. What was unusual in this case was that he cared.

Normally, it was very black and white, and Bryson didn't bother with a witness's fragile emotions. But he'd seen what Jesse had done to some of the other women, had heard their stories — when they were alive to tell them — and he just couldn't make Misty suffer any more than she already had.

The quiet rustle in the bathroom made him aware that Misty was now slipping on the clothes Axel had bought during a run to the local Walmart. They probably weren't the most comfortable, but they'd do for now. Because he and Axel had found Misty, that meant Jesse most likely knew where she was, too.

It was only a matter of time before the man either showed up or sent someone to silence her permanently. That bad cop had to know that his game was almost up — and he knew Misty was going to be the final nail in his coffin.

The only way Bryson could fully protect her was if she agreed to testify, and if her testimony was crucial to the case. He hated the politics, hated that they would have no choice but to leave her to sink or swim if she wasn't useful enough.

Did that make them no better than the dirty cop they were dealing with?

When the door from the bathroom opened, Bryson took a double look. With the heavy makeup she'd sported at the fast-food joint now gone and the dull brown color contacts out, she was breathtaking. Her eyes, which were a little too large for her sunken cheekbones, were definitely her best feature, a compelling dark green with specks of silver shining in them. Her full lips were more relaxed than they'd been earlier, though pointed just a bit downward, and her hair had disappeared into a towel on top of her head.

The clothes were too big, hanging loosely on her small frame, but as she fiddled with the hem of her shirt, he could see that she preferred the larger clothes to something too tight. His colleague had no clue how to shop for women, but it looked as if Axel had done all right.

After taking his time memorizing every single feature on her slim face, he found himself gazing at that luscious mouth. He wouldn't mind taking a taste — just one little taste.

Of course, he wouldn't.

Shaking his head, he looked down and inhaled deeply. This was getting more bizarre by the second. It was time to rein himself in and take care of his witness — not scare her all over again. If she noticed the way he was gazing at her mouth, she was sure to run.

He was acting no better than her ex right now. And to be compared to that man was a definite insult, even if he was doing the comparing himself.

"I hope the shower helped," he said a bit awkwardly after they'd both stood in silence for too long.

"Yes, thank you." She moved over to a chair and sat, pulling her legs up to her chest and hugging them close. Her body language spoke volumes — the telltale signs of someone needing to protect herself.

"Do you want to sleep first, or can you talk?" They had a lot to accomplish and he hoped she'd talk. But he wasn't sure what would be said right now. It was going to take her at least a day or two to trust him.

"What do you want from me?" This time, she looked up, right into his eyes, and he saw a measure of strength that made him oddly happy.

She might be afraid, might be out of her element, but there was a strand of steel running up her spine that was keeping her alive — the only thing, it seemed.

"We need to talk about your ex, Jesse Marcus."

Her eyes narrowed slightly before she suppressed her emotions and took a long intake of oxygen. She paused for a moment to choose her words. She had to be careful not to reveal too much. It was a game — and she intended to be the winner.

She wouldn't give him anything that he didn't drag from her.

"I don't know who you're talking about," she said, lifting her hands and undoing the towel wrapped on her head. The wet strands of her hair fell down past her shoulders, hanging over the front of the knees still pressed up against her chest.

The long, dark brown strands were a perfect complement to her delicate features and green eyes. She was truly a beauty, and after a few months of security, that beauty would be like a beacon on a cold, foggy night, drawing people from near and far.

"Let's make a deal not to lie to each other, Misty. Why don't you make yourself more comfortable by asking me some questions?" He gave her a smooth smile that was supposed to instill trust.

"Where did you come from?" she finally asked.

"I'm based in Montana, but I travel all over the U.S."

"Doing what exactly?"

"I mainly look for major drug dealers, the men and women who are killing people with their product and their 'cutthroat' business practices. I'm not interested in the small-timers, and not in the people who are hurting only themselves or trying to take care of their cancer. The locals can handle them. I like to make sure the big players are all set up in their new homes for the next twenty-five to life."

"You're good at your job, aren't you?"

"Very good." This was an area he was sure of — there weren't any blurred lines. The people were either guilty or not. He'd never found a criminal dealing tons of cocaine who had a valid excuse for breaking the law.

"Obviously, then, you enjoy your job," she said, her shoulders loosening up just a bit as she let go of her hold on her knees. She crossed her legs and began to run her fingers through her hair; fiddling with it seemed to calm her.

"I love my job. It doesn't get much better than stopping the bad guys."

"I can see you're also rather humble," she said, her first hint at a joke. This was progress!

"Yeah, in my line of work, humility is a must," he said, his lips turning up in a blinding grin.

"I remember when I was so impressed with anyone who worked on the so-called right side of the law," she told him with a bitter sigh. "That was before I learned how the world really works."

That knocked him down a peg or two, and his smile faltered. "And how is that, Misty?"

"It isn't the good guys and the bad. There are only those with power — some with too much power. The more they get, the more they want. The more they need. I used to think that when you put on a uniform, strapped on that gun belt and held that badge, it meant you were someone people should look up to. Now I know that's not always the case. Don't get me wrong. There are plenty of men and women who know the sanctity of that uniform, but there are also a lot who use it to get whatever they think they deserve."

"I couldn't agree with you more, Misty. There are a lot of rotten men and women out there. That's why I need your help to keep one of them off the streets. If we lock Jesse up, he can't hurt you, and he can't hurt anyone else either, ever again."

"Do you really believe that?"

"With my entire being."

"How did you find me?"

Ah. Her question revealed that he was getting somewhere. She wasn't denying that she was Misty. Finally.

"It wasn't easy. Took me a long time, but persistence pays off."

"That wasn't an answer. I mean, how did you find *me*? How did you know who I was?"

"I shouldn't divulge my secrets…" he began, but as the shutters began closing over her eyes, he decided to give her this one. "Another agent came in and had lunch at the place you were employed. You were working the counter. Though your disguise is good, we're trained to see past the mask of makeup, the makeshift disguises, and see who is behind it all. He had a good feeling it was you. When he snuck a picture and sent it to me, I knew."

"It was that simple?" Her shoulders slipped, and she stopped combing her hair.

"Hey. It's been almost a year since you disappeared off the face of the planet. I wouldn't exactly call that simple. I've had your picture on my wall that entire time, so I would hope that I could recognize you."

She waited. He hadn't asked her another question. Those green eyes looked somewhere over his shoulder, and he knew she'd rather be any other place than sitting in this room with him. It was time to drop the "good cop" role.

"Are you seeing anyone, Ms. Elton?" Where in the hell had that question come from? It hadn't been what he'd been expecting to say. Her personal life was none of his business, and it certainly had no impact on the case in any way.

"I… What does that matter?" she asked, but he just looked back at her, his expression impassive as he waited for her answer. "No," she finally murmured.

Good. He didn't know why that pleased him — she was a witness, dammit. It would be breaking every sort of ethical rule he knew even to consider asking her out. He'd known the moment he'd asked that question that he was crossing a line. He should have retracted it. But he'd be showing her a chink in his armor, and that wasn't a wise move at this point in the questioning.

"How long did you date Jesse Marcus?" There. That was a legitimate question. At least he was reining himself in.

"It was a while ago, and I'd rather not discuss him." She lifted her hands to fiddle with her hair again. The way she tugged at the strands was a good gauge of her feelings, Bryson found. The faster she pulled, the more distressed she was. When she slowed down, she was relaxing.

He was already learning her moves — learning what made her tick, or at least a part of it —and he'd been with her only a few hours.

She had slender hands. They were also the hands of a woman not afraid to work, not afraid to get her nails dirty or broken, but still, her fingers were slim and pretty, and they looked as if they should be adorned with gold and jewels, not rough from scrubbing pots and pans and using industrial cleaners.

This was now past irrational and into the Twilight Zone. He'd never before had such a difficult time focusing on a witness and on keeping an interrogation going in the right direction. *Pull yourself together.*

"Did you participate in any criminal activities with Mr. Marcus?"

Her head snapped up and fire lit up her eyes. That had certainly pushed a few of her buttons. Good. He didn't want her to be guilty.

"Do I need a lawyer, Mr. Winchester?" Her tone was strong as she once again met his gaze.

Though it was foolish of him, he felt pride for her strength, pride for her ability to stand strong in the midst of all this terror. This woman would *fight* — fight to put Jesse behind bars where he belonged. Bryson just had to convince her that the fight wouldn't kill her, that she could be kept safe.

"You are certainly entitled to one," he said, reaching into his pocket. He saw that the movement made her tense up. Did she honestly think he'd be reaching for his gun? Maybe. That was the only kind of law she was familiar with right now. He'd have to show her that not all men who carried a gun liked to terrorize others.

He pulled out a business card and walked over to her slowly, holding it out, and waiting for her to accept it. "He's good — very good." Bryson stepped back and waited.

She held the card, running her fingers along the edge, across the face, feeling the way the expensive lettering rose from the surface. The lawyer was a personal friend of his, and the man hadn't lost a case in…well…ever, at least that Bryson knew of.

"He's one of the attorneys who have been secured for the witnesses on this case, to answer questions, address concerns, and to take statements when you're ready. He's not on the prosecution's team; he's just offered his services for witness questions. If you don't trust him after you meet, you can get a referral for another attorney, but I'm telling you, he's good, one of the best I know, and I don't trust a lot of lawyers. You don't have to take just the word of our team on this, Misty, but please give him a chance and speak with him."

"I did see some…stuff…"

"That's good, Misty. Tell me what you know," he said, keeping his tone smooth, polite, trustworthy.

"I just don't know if I can do this." Her fingers began to tremble.

"You can, Misty. This is the right thing to do. I'll keep you safe and then that man will never hurt another person again — will never hurt you again." It was a vow he hoped to keep. If his agency said she wasn't needed, his hands would be tied. After only a few hours, he felt a need to keep her protected, and the only way would be if she talked.

She looked up, paused a couple of heartbeats before barely whispering: "Not everything is so black and white. There is very much a gray area when it comes to the law."

Bryson knew this. He hated it, but he was well aware.

"We need to stay on track, Ms. Elton. I think that is wisest." He'd reverted to her last name when he felt a flash of desire to pull her into his arms — to comfort her. *Focus on the freaking job.*

"I agree, Mr. Winchester," she said rigidly. "I'm very tired now, though. Would you mind if we continued tomorrow?"

He wasn't going to get anything else from her tonight. She was finished with talking, and to push it now would probably be pointless.

"Axel will be back at any time with dinner."

"I'm not hungry, but thank you."

She stood up and moved toward the door to her room.

"Ms. Elton," he called out, and though her back stiffened, she turned her head and looked back at him. "I'll be right next door, in the morning."

His last remark was meant to reassure her that she wouldn't be alone, but it was also a warning so she wouldn't try to run.

He was a good guy — he took pride in that. But it would be a mistake to think that made him weak. Bryson had an edge of pure danger running through his veins. He thrived on it. And that's probably what made him one hell of an agent.

CHAPTER FOUR

D O YOU THINK that Jesse Marcus constitutes a threat to your life?"

Misty looked up at the two agents and wondered if they were mentally unstable. How many times and in how many ways had she already told them that Jesse would kill her the first chance he got?

"I know this seems repetitive, Misty, but if we are to put you in the witness protection program, there has to be a direct threat against you. We need this on record that you are in danger," Bryson said, his tone gentle.

"I don't *think* Jesse will try to kill me. I *know* he will, Agent Winchester. Jesse told me that when he was through with me, he'd make sure I was never able to divulge his secrets. He told me he'd killed former girlfriends. He won't hesitate to take my life. I don't want to testify, but if you are going to force me to do this, then I won't agree unless you can guarantee my safety. I think that's a fair trade-off," she said, her arms crossed as she looked at both men.

"We agree. There have been witnesses not in protection who have come up missing. I'm not telling you this to frighten you; I'm telling you because Jesse is not locked up at this point, and you need to be aware of that. You've done an excellent job so far of keeping away from him, but he knows we're closing in. He knows it won't be much longer until we issue the arrest warrant."

"I understand that. But is there any way for me to just continue to hide out until this is all over? Can't you get him behind bars without my testimony?" This would be ideal for her.

"I wish I could, but from what we've found on you so far, we believe that you're a valuable asset to this case. We don't need the whole story right now. We encourage you to speak to your lawyer, look at your options. This process isn't short. It takes months, even years sometimes, but if you want our help, we need you to sign notarized statements that you will testify if you are called upon to do so."

Bryson wasn't being cruel as he sat across the table from her in the local FBI offices. She'd absolutely refused to go to the police station. There was no way Jesse wouldn't hear about exactly where she was if that happened.

She didn't trust the cops, and she barely trusted the FBI. She'd rather this entire mess were behind her, that she was on the other side of it, finally living a somewhat normal life.

"Then what happens if I sign the document?"

"We get you set up in a new location. You use an alias, get a job, go on living your life. We will check in on you, make sure you're fine, and that's where you'll stay until the hearing. When it's over, you can either keep the name, stay in the location, and resume your life as the new person, or you can go back to who you were," Axel said.

"I don't get any time to think about this?"

"I'm sorry, but you need to decide now." They'd already told her this several times.

If she didn't do what they wanted, they were well within their rights to lock her up, and she'd be locked up in a county jail, a place where Jesse would have much easier access to her.

Looking at the two options before her, she decided that testifying was the lesser of evils. Still, speaking to the attorney seemed a really good idea, even if that frightened her, too.

She was so sick and tired of being afraid. How dare Jesse do this to her, make her into such a weak woman? It wasn't okay, not okay at all. She was sick of the men in her life having such power over her. It had been that way since she was a small child.

None of it was her fault, but that's just the fate she'd been handed.

"Fine. I'll sign your piece of paper," she finally said.

"I'm really glad to hear that, Misty," Bryson replied, and their eyes connected for just a moment, a moment that had her stomach tightening.

It wasn't attraction. She couldn't possibly feel that toward him. It was fear. That had to be what it was. She lowered her eyes quickly, unwilling to look too deep.

There was a knock on the door, and then an intern stepped in with their lunch and set it on the table. Misty's stomach rumbled, surprising her. She hadn't eaten in over twenty-four hours, but her nerves had been tied in knots, making it impossible.

Now that she'd made a solid decision, even if it wasn't an ideal solution, her stress levels were actually going down and the thought of food was heavenly.

"I'm going to get the paperwork," Bryson said. He stood and followed the intern out, leaving her sitting there with Axel, who made her much more nervous than Bryson did.

She didn't know why, as he was the one always cracking jokes, but the guy seemed more lethal to her. Maybe it was the almost cold look in his eyes. She just didn't know.

But as he passed her a cheeseburger, fries, and a shake, she made sure not to brush his fingers with hers. After several minutes passed, and her hunger pangs eased, she grew more curious, and she found herself wanting to talk.

"How long have you and Agent Winchester worked together?" Nerves shot through her as he looked over her way. Damn, this guy was intimidating.

Axel stuffed a few fries in his mouth, chewed and swallowed, and then answered her question. "Five years."

Taking a deep breath, she asked him the question of the hour, one she should have already asked.

"Why am I so important in all of this? I don't understand. There must be a hundred — a thousand — other women who would love to testify against Jesse. I just want to live my life, put all of this behind me. I just want to be free of these stupid mistakes I've made." Her voice gained force and clarity during her impassioned speech.

One look from his cold hazel eyes and she backed down. Damn, this man's interrogation tactics must be out of this world.

"Not all cases are so black and white, Misty. The more evidence we obtain on this piece of scum, the more likely we are to lock him up and throw away the key. If he stays on the street wearing a badge — carrying a gun — then no one is safe. Don't you understand that?"

He seemed genuinely perplexed that she wasn't taking this more seriously. It wasn't that she thought it was a joke; it was just that she didn't want to face the giant, and that's what Jesse was to her — a giant man with a giant fist, and an even bigger temper.

It would take Jesse only seconds to kill her. He could have her neck snapped before she ever got the chance to call out for help. He could leap across a table and strangle her before anyone even thought about stopping him. If Jesse knew he was going to jail anyway, what would it matter to him if he killed her? The man was that crazy — crazy enough to get in one last victim before being locked up for good. A courtroom full of witnesses would be neither here nor there to him.

"I don't trust people," she said as she sipped on her vanilla shake. Her stomach was feeling much better now.

"I figured that out when you Tased my partner," he said with a chuckle.

"You didn't seem in a hurry to help him," she countered, feeling only a bit guilty over the whole Taser incident. Bryson *had* grabbed her, after all…

"Nah, Bryson's a tough guy. We've been Tasered before."

Her eyes widened at his words. He'd said them so casually. "You have? Why?" Maybe it was another crazy witness, she thought.

"It's all part of the training," he said casually, as if getting thousands of volts of electricity shot into your body happened all the time.

She shook her head, then continued with the questions.

"Does Bryson ever give up?" She knew the answer before Axel spoke.

"Not once since I've known him, and that's been a lot of years. He *will* win this case. He doesn't know the meaning of losing. We have a powerful attorney who wants Jesse's head on a platter. None of us will stop until that happens."

The victory in his eyes seemed to say the case was already won, though Misty knew that was far from true. For the moment, at least, Jesse was very much free — free to come after her any time he wanted.

The conversation must have been over, because Axel stood and took their garbage to the wastebasket. "I'll be back in a few minutes."

With that, she found herself alone in the interrogation room.

When the two men came back in, everything seemed to move at warp speed. The documents were placed before her, and she was left alone again as she read through them. After an hour, she found there really wasn't a good reason not to sign.

Once she'd turned the papers over, she was escorted outside, transferred to a jet and on her way to her new life with a new identify. Well, a new identity until this was all over.

And no longer than that, she vowed. Because as she sat down in her small home and looked at her new driver's license, with the name Magnolia Linhart and a different date of birth, she knew she didn't want this to be her.

Yes, her life had been anything but perfect, but Misty Elton was who she was; it was the name the children's services department had given her, anyway. It was all she knew, and she didn't want to start again.

This would only be temporary, right?

Misty was about to find out how slowly the wheels of justice turned.

CHAPTER FIVE

A SWEET SMILE flitted across Misty's lips as she lifted her face to the sky and enjoyed the sun beating down upon her. Yes, it was a bit too warm, and, yes, sweat was beading on her neck, but it didn't matter.

This was her second month in her new home, and she finally felt as if she were secure again. She finally felt free to sit out on her front lawn and dig weeds from the flower beds. Up until the week before, she'd gone straight to her part-time job as a graveyard shelf stocker, and straight back home again, too afraid of being outside in the daylight hours.

Fear.

It was real; it made a person fight or flee; it shaped a person; it could mean living or dying. Fear was a constant with Misty, but she wasn't going to let it rule her anymore. She wasn't going to allow Jesse the satisfaction of knowing that even though he was free to do what he pleased, she was locked in a cage.

Bryson had been gone since he and Axel had dropped

her off at her new home, working on finding other witnesses, on building the case. The agent who'd been checking on her was unfamiliar, and unbelievably rigid. The guy made her thoroughly uncomfortable. She just didn't trust strangers — didn't trust anyone, really. So why did she find herself missing Bryson? He was a stranger, too.

She had known him for only a day, and it appalled her to be upset that he was no longer her agent.

It was just that she was depending on him, counting on him. Then, she was suddenly thrust into the care of another agent. It was confusing.

Mystifying her even more had been the phone calls from Bryson to see how she was doing, to make sure she was adjusting. She didn't think it was exactly protocol in these situations if he wasn't her agent anymore, but she didn't have friends, didn't have family, so the shoulder he was offering, even if it was only over the phone, had been too nice for her to turn down.

It had been two weeks since the last time he'd phoned, though. She didn't know if he was in a situation where he couldn't call, or if it simply meant that he'd grown bored with their conversations.

Either way, though she hated to admit it, she missed the sound of his voice. When would she learn to not depend on anyone else but herself?

The lesson clearly hadn't sunken in yet.

Still, something she *had* learned was how to control her fear. Being with Jesse had been forced upon her; she wasn't the one in the wrong in that situation. Once she had accepted that, although the fear was still there, at the back of her senses, she was making a valiant effort to really live — well, live as much as she could while residing in a place that wasn't hers for long.

As the sun rose higher in the sky, Misty's skin turned pink, and she knew she should go back in, since she didn't have sunblock on, but she couldn't make herself do so. She was also strongly considering a haircut, but for some reason she wasn't able to bring herself to have it done. She'd had never felt beautiful, but the only compliment she could ever remember from her childhood had been when her fourth-grade teacher said she loved her hair.

From that moment on, Misty had taken pride in her long, dark tresses, brushing them more gently, from the bottom to the top, the way one foster mom had shown her, and braiding her hair loosely at night so it would have a pretty curl to it in the morning.

Still, with the sun beating down, she wouldn't have minded having a little less hair at this particular moment. But she'd rather be too hot, enjoying the sun, than stuck back inside the small, lonely house.

Dumping water on her shoulders gave her instant relief. It cooled her down just enough that she could get at least another half hour in her front garden before she had to drag herself back in or risk heat stroke.

Digging her hand shovel happily into the ground, she pulled at another root, hoping she'd still be here to see the roses bloom next month. Lifting her hand, she ran her finger gently across one of the stems, feeling the sharpness of a thorn.

It made her smile. No matter how beautiful roses were,

they could cause a lot of pain. That concept worked for people as well. Though Special Agent Bryson Winchester was a very beautiful male, he could certainly inflict a lot of damage.

She'd learned that from the conversations the two of them had shared. His voice over the phone was no less masculine, was no less sexy, than he was. The man had sensual energy seeping through his skin, and the phone line seemed only to accelerate the speed with which those waves reached her.

After grabbing her shears, she was cutting away dead debris when she heard a vehicle pull up to the curb alongside her house. Heart racing, Misty found herself frozen, though that reaction ticked her off, especially after she'd delivered that lecture to herself on bravery. Much as she struggled to relax her muscles, however, she couldn't seem to turn her head, to reassure herself that it was just a neighbor, simply someone who lived next door and was returning home.

Her fear wasn't quite as much under control as she'd hoped.

"Breathe," she whispered, then forced her head to inch upward. When she spotted the long, lean legs encased in a pair of fitted jeans, her breath whooshed out in relief, and then she tensed for a completely different reason.

As her eyes continued to travel upward, they rose over the light green polo, and she locked gazes with Bryson Winchester. Nope. Two months of not seeing him had done nothing to her libido. She was just as affected by him now as she was the first time they'd met. If not more.

Only this time, she wasn't afraid.

Running a hand through the escaped tendrils of her damp hair, Misty was suddenly self-conscious about the way she was dressed. She looked down to see dirt-caked hands and grass stains on her clothes. It shouldn't matter — but somehow it did.

Walking up to her, Bryson didn't say a word, his eyes intense, a smile flitting across his lips. Misty wondered whether she would find her voice in the next few moments, before the situation became any more awkward.

"What are you doing here?" she finally asked, her voice a bit too breathy.

He seemed to be taking his sweet time answering, and Misty was feeling a whole new kind of heat creeping down her neck. Her stomach tensed. How it was that she felt any kind of attraction toward this man? Men weren't trustworthy. Not even this special agent who'd saved her from Jesse — for now.

He wasn't here on a social call. This would be business. That's all the two of them had together. Even if he were making a social call, it wouldn't matter. She wasn't interested in a relationship — she just wanted to live her life without drama. Without men.

Someday, that might be possible.

"My supervisor sent me. We've gathered all the witnesses and I've now been reassigned to you," he finally replied as he squatted down, putting himself at eye level with her, and making her feel at a huge disadvantage.

The surge of disappointment from his answer irritated her.

Of *course* he was here on business. She'd already known that. It changed nothing. She'd just been telling herself that they would never be anything to each other but casual acquaintances. When this was all over, she would never see him again.

The clothes he was wearing weren't bought at a cheap department store, and so, even if she *had* been interested in dating, he was way beyond her league. This man wouldn't be seen out socially with a woman like her. It just didn't happen.

She stood up slowly, feeling uncomfortable remaining on her knees. "What happened to Agent Benson?"

"He's been assigned to another case."

"What if I don't want to change agents?" she challenged him, her bravery rising as she faced him. She had managed to get the upper hand on him once, she remembered with some pleasure.

"Then I'd have to say, 'Tough,' Misty." His smile turning up a notch, making her take a cautious step backward as her hand lifted again and she wiped the sweat from her brow.

Great! Now she was going to have a streak of mud on her forehead. This just kept getting better by the second.

"Well, I could say, 'Tough,' when you ask me questions." Feeling at a disadvantage, she was consequently acting slightly immature.

His smile grew even bigger, and he winked. "I have ways of making a witness talk."

"I guess that just makes you *special*," she quipped, hating the way he was perfectly unaffected by her stubbornness. She could sense her own irritation growing by leaps and bounds.

He leaned forward, invading her personal bubble. "I could show you exactly how *special* I am," he whispered.

Whoa! That was definitely not professional. What was he trying to do now? Seduce her into talking, giving him what he wanted, obviously. She just needed to remember that's all this was about — her testimony.

She finally broke the long silence that followed. "Um…it's getting pretty hot out here. I was just finishing up," she said. Better just to let him win their verbal battle.

"Great. I'm a bit warm myself." He stood up and invited himself to join her. She wasn't sure how she felt about that, but for some reason she couldn't seem to tell him to go away.

"I really have a lot to do…"

"How about we start this conversation again?" he asked with a killer smile. "I'm in town working, and thought I'd stop by. It's been a long drive, and my throat is parched."

Misty stood there for a moment, and then, unbidden, her lips twitched at his blatant hint. This man knew how to be charming, knew how to get his way. She'd bet he killed it on the stand when he testified as an expert witness.

"I made a fresh pot of iced tea a little while ago," she told him, the idea of sitting with a cool drink with this man was too dang appealing for her liking.

"Perfect. I just so happen to love tea." He held out his arm to escort her inside.

Misty looked at the arm for a moment, then looked down, pretending she hadn't noticed his gesture. She bent down and gathered her gardening tools, placed them in the basket she was using, and began walking toward her front door.

She could swear she heard him chuckle, but when she turned her head, his mouth was closed, though there was a smile on his lips. Maybe she was just getting paranoid at this point.

When his hand brushed her back as they reached the front door, a chill slithered down her body, a tingling chasing that sensation. One small touch and she was heated and cooled all at once. Never before could she remember reacting this way to a guy — not her first lover, and certainly not Jesse.

Drawing away from him, she slipped inside the door while giving herself a stern lecture. *You will not feel a response to this man. He is trying to manipulate you into doing what he wants. This is all pointless. He will disappear in a few minutes, and then you probably won't ever see him again, so pull yourself together.*

The mental lecture seemed to help...a little. The sooner she gave Bryson a drink and then ushered him back out her front door, the better for her racing heart and her suddenly reawakened libido.

Now get busy. Misty went straight to the cupboard and pulled out a couple of glasses, then filled them with ice and sweetened iced tea. Next, she grabbed a box of cookies and then moved over to the table.

It wasn't as if she'd had a lot of visitors — none, actually other than Agent Benson, when he was checking in with her. She hadn't been very social with that man at all. OK, there was also the guy with the dog, but he didn't come inside.

"Great iced tea," Bryson said.

"Thanks. I just followed the directions on the box."

His smile was distracting her. Even though she knew she was saying the wrong things, knew she should be less tense, he seemed more fascinated by her than appalled. He was either one hell of an actor or he just didn't get out much.

In any case, they weren't exactly a match made in heaven.

Not that she should be thinking of them as a match or a pair, or anything at all that involved two people. They were simply strangers. It was very black and white.

"I have to say, I really like how you've done up the place. I've seen a lot of temp homes in my years on the team, and people usually don't do much with them. They prefer to get out as soon as possible. You've made this place really homey."

Misty tried to look around the small space through his eyes. It wasn't much, a small three-bedroom, two-bathroom home, but still much too large for just her, much larger than she was used to. The walls were sparsely decorated, and the furnishings minimal. Against all odds, though, she'd grown quite attached.

After she finally started to leave the house during daylight hours, she'd managed to find a craft store and had picked up a few painting supplies, so the walls now had a couple of amateur pictures with large splashes of color on them, and a cross-stitch project was sitting on the coffee table.

She'd never done one before, but she'd been excited to try something new. It wasn't going well, but depending on how long she was living there, she might just be able to master the craft eventually.

"I like it here. It's a great town, not far from the city, but the neighborhood is friendly. Mr. Whistler down the street usually stops and chats with me for a few minutes while he's walking his little dog. I swear that thing is a terror, though. I tried to pet him once, and he nearly took a finger off."

He laughed. "Don't tell me that you're afraid of a little tiny dog!"

"Just because they're little doesn't mean their teeth aren't sharp. They could latch on to a vein and bleed you dry."

Bryson gazed at her for a moment as if trying to determine whether she was serious or not. When she realized how ridiculous she sounded, she smiled just a bit. Bryson had no idea that when she'd been ten, a medium-sized dog had attacked her, leaving a scar on the back of her leg. The thing had *really* latched on.

That had been her first experience with a tetanus shot. The darned needle had been so large that she was sure the people who had invented the dosage had secretly been fiendish villains, out to torture young people stupid enough to need the dang injection.

"I think we've all had frightening experiences with dogs. When I was about eight, I was riding my bike in our neighborhood. It was dusk, and I knew that if I didn't get home in less than five minutes, my mom was going to whip me, so I was hauling down a hill and I wiped out. I'm lying there, trying real hard not to cry while blood was gushing from my elbow, and right then this mean-assed boxer shows up. I was an idiot and started running. He nipped me right in the behind. I think he was just herding me, though, 'cause the skin didn't break. I just had one giant-sized bruise, making it hard to sit for the next week or so."

She didn't know how he could laugh about such a frightening experience, but she did know she probably would have done the same and run like crazy. Of course, in her case, with her luck, the dang dog would have jumped her, pinned her down, and eaten her for dinner.

Just when Misty found herself beginning to relax, she stiffened right back up. It wouldn't help to not stay on guard. "Really, Bryson, what are you doing here?"

There was no need to act coy. He'd eventually have to get to the reason for his visit. She had no clue where he lived, but it most likely wasn't close, so he *had* to have gone out of his way for this visit, even if he was in his regular clothes. That was probably just to reassure her that he was just an average Joe.

"It's time for your testimony. There are only a few witnesses left who haven't made their depositions, so we need to lock down the schedule." He connected their gazes, refusing to release her from the pull of his eyes.

It felt like trying to escape from a spider's web. She shook her head. She literally had to bite her tongue to keep from telling him he could have her. No wonder she was an easy victim. It didn't take much to make her fall under a smooth man's spell.

"The last time we spoke, I told you I needed more time." It seemed the FBI didn't like that answer.

Another smile. He shifted, as if trying to get more comfortable. At least he broke eye contact while doing it. With one ankle now resting on his knee, he smiled yet again, his perfectly straight teeth gleaming in the natural sunlight pouring in through the windows.

"Have you called the attorney yet, spoken with Camden?" he asked.

"No. Since you were the one who recommended him, I don't see how I can trust that he won't just tell me what you want me to hear."

Bryson chuckled, seeming to enjoy their sparring. Her body relaxed involuntarily, and she leaned back and lifted her glass, her tongue darting out to run along the rim. She took full advantage of the coolness in her hands.

When his eyes darkened instantly, her own widened. Wow. The tension was back, and it was so thick, it could be cut with a paring knife.

"I have another card here. You have Internet access, right?" She nodded her head. "Yes."

"Good. Then run a search on the guy. He's in Montana, where the case is being tried, but I know he'll be willing to come down here and speak with you. Yes, he wants this bastard behind bars as much as I do, but he won't lie to you, won't falsify information to get what he wants. I won't, either."

"Couldn't I just talk to him on the phone?" The thought of having another man come to her place didn't please her. This was her haven, and she didn't want to share it.

"We could go up there," he suggested, as if he had read her mind.

"Wouldn't that be unsafe?" That was where Jesse was. Going back there wouldn't be good for her piece of mind.

"How about we meet at a neutral location down here?"

"Why do you have to be there? I can't get honest answers if you're there," she said, and for just a second, so quickly that she knew she had to have imagined it, hurt flashed across his face.

Then, in a blink, his smile reappeared.

"Of course. I will set it up but stay back. I want you to feel confident after the meeting with him. His name is Camden Whitman, and he's been a friend of mine for over fifteen years.

You can trust this man with your life."

She saw truth shining in his eyes, but how well did anyone really know anyone else? Bryson might think that he could trust this lawyer, but why did he feel that way? The more pressing question was this: Why did she feel as if she could trust Bryson? She didn't want to, and she had her guard up, but the bottom line was that she thought he was telling her the truth. Or at least her gut told her he was speaking the truth — not that her gut had always led her in the right direction.

Maybe it would clarify things if she just met with the lawyer, got it out of the way. She'd agreed to testify, so putting off the next step was only postponing the inevitable. Besides, if she could help get Jesse off the streets, how many women would that save? How many people would sleep better at night?

Sipping her tea, she glanced up, trying to be casual, hoping to gauge his expression without his noticing. Nope. His eyes were still locked on her as he sat there — quite still — not saying anything more. Just waiting on her.

"I guess it wouldn't hurt to talk to him…"

"Great!"

For some odd reason, she liked that she'd pleased him. This was another bad sign.

"What happens if Jesse doesn't go to prison?"

This was the ultimate fear. If she got on that stand, testified against him, let him know how much she really knew about him, and then somehow the justice system failed and he was released, she had no doubt that Jesse would never stop coming after her. He was the sort of man who could never allow a woman to betray him without seeking what he deemed justice in his sick mind.

"Then I will shoot him myself." The level look in Bryson's eyes let her know he meant what he said.

The thought was almost as frightening to her as it was of Jesse being free.

This man, sitting so nonchalantly at her kitchen table, wearing a light-colored shirt, drinking a glass of her tea, had killed before. She had no doubt about it.

"Wouldn't that make you just as wrong as him?"

He looked at her, some of the coldness leaving his eyes before he answered. "He would leave me no choice, Misty. I wouldn't shoot him in the back. But he would go after you, after all of the witnesses, and I would be left with no choice but to take his life."

His words were spoken so matter-of-factly. It was just another day on the job. Misty had no idea how people could reach a point in their life where they could talk of such a thing as killing another so cavalierly, as if they were discussing nothing more meaningful than peanut butter and jelly. But Bryson had obviously reached that point.

There was no turning back.

"It's never easy to take a life, but sometimes it has to be done for the greater good of society," he told her.

She got that, even believed in the death penalty, but she didn't think she could be the one to flip the switch in the execution room, didn't think she'd be able to fire the weapon.

"You think you wouldn't be able to do it, but you'd be surprised what you can do when the will to survive is at its greatest," he said, shocking her. "I can't read minds, if that's what you're worried about. I can just read your thoughts through your eyes."

"I guess that's something I need to work on."

"Don't change it." His voice was passionate, and he leaned forward, his mouth mere inches from her own. She licked her lips as she glanced down, and that feeling in her stomach ratcheted up tenfold this time.

When he cleared his throat, she jerked back, realizing she'd been lusting after him.

"I really should get a few chores done before I go to sleep. I have to work tonight," she murmured, feeling suddenly claustrophobic in her own house.

"I'll leave for now, but I'll be back soon," he promised, or threatened — however she chose to look at it. At this point, she had no clue.

All she really knew was that she needed to get her wits together.

Bryson stood, and she didn't realize that he'd walked out the front door until she heard his vehicle start. After getting shakily to her feet, she moved to the front window, and then their gazes met through the glass pane of the passenger side window, leaving her standing there frozen. He smiled, turned away, and pulled away from the curb onto the quiet street.

The fates seemed to be forever against her, so she'd bet every last dime she had to her name, which wasn't much, that preparations for this trial were going to drag on for a long time, a very long time, leaving this man almost a fixture in her life.

Sliding to the floor with her glass clutched tightly in her fingers, Misty groaned.

Yes, a very long time, she thought again. Trials and tribulations.

Gardening time was over. Right now, she had to cool off, and then she had an attorney to speak to.

CHAPTER SIX

Misty's nerves were stretched thin as she walked into the luxurious hotel and looked around at the gleaming lobby. Men and women seemed to be gliding across the polished slate flooring on their way to the high front desk.

She felt woefully underdressed in her plain black skirt and white top, certain that she stood out like a broken finger around these men in hand-tailored suits and women in dresses that cost many times what her last car had. None of the attire could be purchased at the local mall — that was certain.

This had been a mistake — stepping into a world where she didn't belong. This was the sort of place people with money frequented. People with *serious* money.

Her fingers shaking, she turned her head and looked toward the doors. It wasn't too late to escape. Sure, Camden Whitman had flown in from Montana to meet with her, but he would probably be relieved if she didn't show. How useful could a girl like her really be to this case? Yes, a girl. She felt like a girl, not a woman.

Misty was sure that if they did put her on the stand, she'd fail epically. Yes, she was capable of answering a few questions, but when the cross-examination started, who was to say she wouldn't immediately fall to pieces?

"Ms. Elton?"

Misty froze, fear in her eyes. She wasn't Ms. Elton here. That wasn't her name. She was… What was her name again? It wasn't used all that often, and she easily forgot. Oh, yes, Magnolia Linhart. She shouldn't acknowledge the person addressing her.

"I'm sorry. It's Ms. Linhart, isn't it?"

Yeah, this person knew who she was. Turning, Misty caught sight of a dark gray suit with a splash of blue against a stark white shirt. She tilted her head, up, and up, and up.

Then she was meeting the icy blue eyes of one of the most stunning men she'd ever seen before. Were all the males on this case required to have a certain *GQ* look? This was absurd. His dark blond hair was cut short but styled in a way that only the rich could afford, his jaw solid, chiseled, masculine, and his mouth — wow, that mouth must have inspired many nights of fantasies for more than a few ladies.

She gulped and remained standing in front of him, stock still and utterly speechless.

"I'm Camden Whitman," he said, and he held out his hand.

Common manners kicked in and Misty found her arm rising and then her small hand was clasped in his for a few seconds as she swallowed her natural fear of having a new man take hold of her — even in such an innocent fashion.

When she didn't get any predatory vibes from the contact, she began to relax. Maybe it was foolish, but she was starting to realize that not all men wanted to hurt her, especially not the men she'd met lately, like the FBI agents and the U.S. marshals.

Misty blew out a breath of relief. She could do this. It was just a simple conversation, after all.

"Hi. I'm Mis…" she started to say, before correcting herself. "Magnolia Linhart."

His eyes twinkled, since she'd just made the same mistake as he had, and she felt even better. He didn't seem to be a monster, though, of course, Jesse hadn't seemed to be a monster either. Was her radar for fiends completely broken? But here she was, ready to meet with this man, ready to get some questions answered.

"I'm so glad you agreed to meet with me. I've been working on this…project for a while now, spoken to several women, and a few men. May we go upstairs for privacy?"

Misty tensed again. He wanted to be alone with her? Why? As she looked around, noticing that several pairs of eyes were on them, she understood, but she didn't have to like it. *What if*… No! She *had* to stop thinking like that.

She finally spoke. "That would be fine."

He held out a hand to lead her toward the elevators.

"I hope you found the hotel easily enough," he said as he pushed the elevator to go up.

"Yes, I took a cab." The beautiful gold doors slid open, and she walked inside with him. When the doors shut, she found herself all alone with this stranger, but nothing in her was on red alert. She was nervous, but she didn't feel as if she were in danger.

Her danger signals could be broken, but she didn't think so right now. Anyway, everyone had to go at some point, right? If it was her time, then so be it.

The doors opened onto one of the higher floors, and again Camden gestured for her to precede him. She stepped out, and then he was walking beside her until he stopped at a double door and inserted his key card.

Once she was inside the luxurious suite, her eyes popped out at such extravagance. This room seemed to be larger than the house she was currently hiding in. It was certainly a lot nicer, with the mahogany trim, plush cream carpeting, and distinctive high-end furniture.

"Would you like something to drink?"

"Yes, please." She wouldn't be able to speak unless she wet her throat.

"Have a seat over there. I'll surprise you," he said. She sat on the couch in the sitting area and crossed her legs, then uncrossed them, smoothed out her skirt, and crossed them again.

"Here you are."

Misty took the glass from his fingers, noting the red liquid inside it. Wine. It really was too early for a glass of wine, but with her nerves at the breaking point, one glass didn't sound like such a bad idea. It wasn't as if she had to drive back home, anyway, so a slight buzz might make this meeting go just a little smoother. She lifted the glass to her mouth, then nearly sighed as the liquid glided across her tongue.

"I want you to take a moment and get your bearings before I proceed with my inquiries," Camden said as he sat in the chair directly across from her. "Before I even start, today is informal. We aren't taking notes or recording the conversation. I want for you and me to talk, to get to know each other, mainly to see if you can trust me enough with your story. As of now, it's just the two of us having a conversation. Now, you can ask anything you want. There are no stupid questions."

As she listened to Camden speak, some of the weight was lifted from her chest. No notepads were out, no little machine with a red light blinking. This felt more like a couple of people chatting. She could do this.

"Have I been a suspect?" Misty didn't know why that was the first question to pop out, but she wanted to know.

He paused for a moment, seeming to consider what he was going to say. "We had Jesse under surveillance for several months before you left town, and we'd pretty much eliminated you as a suspect," he began, then paused. "And then you disappeared. At first we thought there might be foul play, but once we got witness testimony of the fight you had, and once we spoke with several people who had seen that you left without Jesse pursuing you, we suspected you'd gone underground. So, yes, anyone dealing with Jesse is a suspect, but you were quickly eliminated from that unhappy group."

"You spoke to my neighbors?" That somehow felt like a violation.

"Yes. You are almost a ghost, Misty." He paused briefly. "Is it okay if I call you Misty?"

"Yes," she murmured. She didn't like her alias name — it

was uncomfortable for her to use or to hear others using. It wasn't as if she were particularly attached to her real name; it was just that she was used to it. During the last year, she'd had a difficult time using her first fake name, and now she was doing it all over again with a completely new one.

"Great. As I was saying, you are almost a ghost. There's very little information on you. No credit, no family, no trails. It wasn't easy to find you."

What shocked Misty was the tone of his voice. He sounded…impressed. That didn't seem possible. It wasn't as if she'd done anything spectacular. She just had no one who cared where she was.

If that were something to brag about, she'd receive the Olympic metal for her efforts. The good thing with having no ties had been that it was easier to leave at a moment's notice. The bad thing was that she had no one to turn to when the chips were stacked against her.

"I was raised in the foster-care system. I don't know anyone, really — don't have any deep connections."

Something in his eyes softened. Sympathy. She was used to that, and couldn't stand it. What would a person like him know about it, anyway? He had no right to be sympathetic toward her.

"I was in the foster-care system, too, Misty, until I was nine. Then I was lucky enough to meet my father."

Wow. Misty stared at this professional man before her, with his custom suit, a sparkle in his eyes, and confidence screaming from every pore. He'd been a foster kid? It didn't seem possible.

"You can't just accept your fate, Misty. I had given up, as so many others do. But you can be whoever and whatever you want. That's why it's so important that you stand up against this villain who took advantage of you, used you, and made you run. Jesse Marcus took something from you, and now it's time for you to take it back. I can tell you that when you testify, you will start to put the pieces of your life back together, or better yet, make a whole new life that is even better than it was before. The fear will dwindle, and you can pull yourself out of this prison you've been forced into."

Misty listened to him speak, his words like molasses warming on top of a hot gas stove, coating her, comforting her, offering her a place to go in a safer world. Oh, this man was clearly a pretty great attorney. She'd bet he didn't ever lose a case. Okay, maybe that was statistically almost impossible, but she'd still bet he hadn't lost in a very long time. He didn't seem capable of it.

"What will I have to do? Will Agent Winchester be involved?"

"Yes, he will be involved all the way through, which is in your favor. I've known Bryson for many years, and he's a solid and a good man. You want him to be on your side. He keeps his word. The only thing that would stop him from protecting you would be death, and I'm telling you, I think he's superhuman, because he's been in a few situations from which no man should have come out alive, and yet he's still here," Camden said with a chuckle.

"So what do you need from me?" she asked again, since he'd either ignored the question or gotten distracted.

"Do you know what a deposition is?"

"No." She didn't know any of this lawyer speak.

"I will meet with you and Agent Winchester and the lead attorney on the case against Jesse in my offices in Montana with a court-appointed recorder taking notes. You will make a legally binding statement, explaining everything you know about Jesse and his criminal dealings. We have a lot of witnesses, Misty. We just want this case to be open-and-shut. Not all the witnesses will be called to the stand, and not all of the statements will be used in the trial unless we think we are losing."

"That's it? I just make a statement?" That wasn't so bad, not at all the way she thought it would be. No Jesse in the room; nobody staring daggers at her.

"I don't want to mislead you, Misty," he said, leaning forward in his chair, his elbows propped up on his knees, his eyes intense. "There is a very *real* chance that we *will* call you to the stand, that we *will* ask you to repeat your story in front of a jury. From the evidence we've found, you seem to know a lot. There are a couple of other women who saw even worse crimes committed by Jesse, but you're a valuable witness. What is going down is a very big prosecution with some even bigger players than Jesse involved, and all testimony is valuable to the case."

Misty gazed back at Camden — this man whom she normally would never have a conversation with, someone she'd pass on the street and not feel worthy enough to nod to, and it gave her a measure of pride that *he* needed *her*. Yes, what he needed her for was her testimony, but that didn't matter. All that mattered right now was that she was needed.

Her entire attitude changed. Not only could she do this, but she *wanted* to do this.

"When will it begin?" she asked. She couldn't get out of this anyway, so she might as well accept it. The sooner it was over, the better.

"Soon. Probably a week or two. But for right now I'd like for you to tell me your story." He leaned back.

"Just start talking?"

"Yes. No pressure, no one recording anything. Remember, this is informal today. We're getting to know each other. You tell me your story, and then I'll advise you of what comes next."

"Okay," Misty said, and she began. She would tell this stranger everything she knew about Jesse, everything she'd been an unwilling witness to during the year she'd been with him. A relatively short period of her life had shaped her more than she cared to admit, and telling this man about it was oddly freeing.

CHAPTER SEVEN

H IS DOORBELL RANG at close to two in the morning, and Bryson didn't even blink. He'd been waiting for this visit.

"You could have at least phoned me and let me know what in the hell was going on!" he snapped as he threw open the door, standing there in his sweats, a pronounced scowl on his face.

"It's good to see you, too, Bryson," Camden said cheerily as he stepped over the threshold of Bryson's temporary home.

"I'm really not in the mood for small talk, Cam. What happened?"

"I think it's better if you wait until the deposition, but what's important is that she is feeling much better about testifying. I'd prefer not to put her on the stand. I think she's strong, but this woman has been put through hell, and I mean the deepest, darkest depths of hell. I really don't want to drag her back there, but I'm pretty sure she can handle it if it comes to that."

Camden walked over to Bryson's liquor cabinet and helped himself.

"I don't want to do that to her, either, Cam. I want to protect her. But to hear it coming from you, a lawyer who will do anything to win — well, I'm surprised." Bryson joined his friend and poured himself a strong drink.

Camden ignored Bryson's lawyer barb. "Hmm. I've never heard you say you didn't want a witness to testify. Are you breaking your own rules and getting involved?" His eyes were twinkling.

"Butt out, Cam," Bryson growled.

Camden laughed outright. "Whoa, this girl has you tied in knots."

"That's impossible. I hardly know her," Bryson snarled, but his temper immediately dissipated, and he slumped into the nearest chair, suddenly exhausted.

"You may hardly know her, but I don't think I've ever seen you this twisted up. Damn! Glad I came here to see this for myself instead of making an impersonal phone call." Camden sat down across from him, looking far too smug for Bryson's liking.

"I just…she's different." Why couldn't he put his finger on what he was feeling?

"She most certainly is. If you aren't interested…" Camden trailed off, but his message was perfectly clear.

"If you touch her, I will break both your legs."

"You could try," Camden replied, fully unperturbed, while Bryson felt as if he were walking a high wire and about to fall off — with no safety net anywhere.

"You're enjoying this, aren't you, Cam? I thought you were on my side." Bryson jumped out of his seat and went over for a refill. This night was growing worse by the minute.

Camden and Misty had been at the meeting for far too long. Bryson had been pacing the house for hours, imagining all sorts of scenarios. For one, Camden was known as a lady-killer. Bryson trusted Camden to be professional, and it would ruin the case if his friend slept with a possible witness, but then again, Bryson also had no business sleeping with a woman he was charged with helping to protect. He could lose everything over it. For another, Camden didn't know how Bryson felt. Well, obviously the guy did now!

"Wow. I could lie and say I'm not enjoying it at all," Cam said, "but lawyers have a bad enough reputation for not being able to tell the truth, so I'll be honest and say that your pain is my absolute delight. I can't ever recall you so messed up over a woman. I do remember, in college, a Sandy something, and you wanting in her pants pretty desperately, but even that doesn't compare to the mess you are in right now."

"Yeah, if I remember right, you scored with Sandy first," Bryson said. He didn't care at all about that old college flame, but he felt he had to point out his friend's horning in on what Bryson had dibbed his.

"Hey, you were the one who made the bet to see which of us could get her out on a date first." Though Cam was defending himself, he was not proud of what an ass he had been back in college.

"She was the one known for chasing only the rich boys," Bryson said, but he was also feeling guilty about the way they'd treated girls back then.

Women had been nothing more than a night of pleasure to them, and once the night was over, the guys had walked away shame-free. As he sat there, he realized that not much had changed in ten years. Pretty pathetic.

"Seriously, Cam, this topic is depressing the hell out of me. Why don't you just tell me what you can, and then we'll get some sleep and forget all about anything else that's been said."

Cam thought for a moment before nodding his agreement. "She was scared when I first approached her, very jumpy. By the end of the night, it was almost like watching a butterfly spread its wings. Something came over her, and confidence shone from her eyes. I was impressed, and you know that doesn't happen too often with me."

"No. You're a very hard man to impress," Bryson said with a chuckle, feeling oddly pleased, and proud of Misty's transformation from the shrinking violet he'd first met. Of course, he had no right to feel those emotions toward his witness. She wasn't his — didn't want to be his — couldn't be his.

It didn't matter how many times he told himself this, he still wanted her, wanted her to the point that she was almost an obsession. It was irrational, and it was the reason he hadn't allowed himself any physical contact with her in two months, until just a few days ago. He'd practically jumped to take the other case. And then he'd done nothing but think about her, and he'd eagerly agreed to go right back to watching over Misty.

Not seeing her for all that time hadn't helped, not even a little. Her voice had come through the phone line sounding all sexy and deep, sending his imagination into overdrive. The worst part of the entire situation? That he knew she wasn't trying to be seductive, wasn't trying to lure him to her. Her innocence was a flipping aphrodisiac — far more effective than chocolate or oysters. Being away from her hadn't done anything to lessen his obsession. If anything, as he discovered when he saw her again after so long, it had only made the coals red-hot.

He'd never before so desired to grab a woman, throw her down on the kitchen table, and show her how high he could make her fly. He'd wanted to bury himself within her, make her scream out his name. He'd wanted to claim her as his...and he still wanted to.

Damn! Now he was getting hard, and this wasn't the time or place. If Cam got even a hint, he'd pounce with his rapier wit. Humiliating. Bryson sat back down.

"Go on," he said, taking a long swallow from his glass.

Cam's eyes were suspicious, but he didn't call Bryson out on his pathetic behavior.

"Her testimony would help seal the case. It's just that her situation sucked."

"Sucked? Really, Cam? Is that official lawyer speak?"

"Shut up, Bryson. I'm trying to put it in layman's terms for your benefit," Cam fired back.

"Okay, okay, enough shots at each other. You're sure she's going to cooperate?" Bryson was worried that she'd take off at the last minute. She was damn good at hiding, and they might not find her again until it was too late. Then he'd have to bust her. And that was the last thing he wanted to do.

"Yes, she'll testify. We will meet and get her official statement. If I can keep her off the witness stand, I will, but I don't think that can happen. There are a few more balls that need to be gathered up before we make the official charge. It doesn't help that Jesse now knows what is happening. All of the witnesses are under protection of U.S. marshals, not to mention us, and he's becoming desperate. That concerns me."

Bryson's stomach tensed. If Camden was worried, there was a problem. "My supervisor is aware of Jesse's activities and he's given us the same information. There is nothing more dangerous than a hunted animal, and that's what Jesse is right now. The boss has assigned me to stay close to here. Axel is covering one of the other witnesses, but we're communicating daily."

"A few minutes could be the difference between life and death," Camden warned him.

"What in the hell am I supposed to do? Move in with her?"

"Yeah, I somehow don't think that will help. You could easily get blindsided when the perp comes in and you're lying on top of her, oblivious to the world."

Suddenly Bryson was in his friend's face. "Don't talk about her that way."

When Cam began laughing, Bryson realized what a fool he was making of himself. He immediately backed off, hoping to recover the situation.

"Whoa, you have it bad," Cam said between chuckles.

"What in the hell is this girl doing to me?" Bryson asked. "We haven't even kissed." He was unusually perplexed. "She's a witness; she's crucial to this trial. I can't screw this up — I've never screwed it up before." He ran a hand through his already mussed hair.

"We all fall eventually, my friend," Cam said, rising to his feet.

"Neither of us has," Bryson reminded him.

"I wouldn't be so sure about that," Cam said, his eyes losing focus for a minute, as if he were no longer in the room with Bryson.

"Now *I'm* curious," Bryson said, on red alert.

"It doesn't matter. Just an old flame."

"I've known you for fifteen years, Cam. If something is tying you up, it won't stop until you fix the situation. You've always had a killer instinct about people, which is what makes you the best damn lawyer I've ever had the pleasure of working with."

It was a rare moment when the two men let down their guard and spoke honestly. Sometimes, being a man wasn't easy — always trying to play the hero, always doing what was expected. Feelings just weren't allowed.

"Let's just get through one case at a time," Cam said. "We'll lock this bastard up for good, and then we can worry about our pathetic love lives."

"I hear you and agree," Bryson told him.

"I need to fly back early, so I'm going to catch a nap and then head out. You fly up next week, and we'll get her testimony on record, then catch dinner at my place before you rush away."

"I've had your cooking, Cam. I'd rather live."

"I agree! We'll go out, Bryson."

"Sounds like a plan. This should be an interesting trip."

The two men parted, and Bryson climbed the stairs of

his temporary home. The next week was going to be hell. He would just have to make sure he kept it professional. Of course he'd do that. He *was* a professional, after all. Having reassured himself on that point, he got into the shower.

Yes, he would put his feelings over this girl on the back burner — keep it neutral — do the job he was hired to do.

It was easier said than done, he knew when he was lying in bed an hour later, thinking of Misty each time he shut his eyes.

"Aw, hell," he muttered as he twisted onto his side and punched his pillow into a usable headrest. He finally fell asleep, and his dreams were filled with one green-eyed beauty and her killer body.

CHAPTER EIGHT

THE DAY WASN'T going as planned, and not only did Bryson have a wicked headache that was threatening to make the top of his skull explode, but he was also running late and worried about Misty. The marshal had flown with her to Montana, and he had come in later.

Dammit.

He'd wanted to fly with her. Maybe his supervisor had realized that...maybe they knew he was feeling less than professional with her. That wouldn't be good for his career. The problem was that he didn't give a lick about his career at the moment.

Right there was a reason he should avoid this woman. She was making him not care about matters that had always been important to him. When a woman wanted a man to change, that was the time to get as far from her as possible.

Okay, the problem wasn't her. It was him. She didn't even know he was having these inappropriate thoughts, and she hadn't tried to change him. It was just happening. He couldn't even think straight.

Walking into his friend's law office, he tried to look at the place through Misty's eyes. This would all be incredibly intimidating for her. His friend was successful. He could have been working in D.C., New York, Seattle, L.A. — pretty much anywhere he wanted. Camden was that good, but he'd chosen to work close to home.

The residents of Montana were more than happy to have him. Camden might look like a pro football player, but the man had a mind more sharp and quick than anyone Bryson had come across. A twinge of jealousy hit as Bryson wondered what Misty thought about his friend. A lot of the girls fell over themselves to get Cam to notice them.

Bryson found himself picking up his pace to get to her. She'd been alone with Cam long enough. And as much as he tried to lie to himself, the truth was that it had been a couple of weeks since he'd last seen her and he couldn't wait to be with her again. If anyone was going to break the rules with this woman, it would be him — not Cam.

"Good evening, Agent Winchester. It's good to see you again," Cam's secretary said. "Mr. Whitman and Ms. Elton will be in conference room C in just a few moments if you'd like to head on in."

"Thank you, Charlotte," Bryson said as he passed by her desk, then walked down the wide hallway. He'd been there often enough to know his way around.

Once in the room, Bryson surveyed the sterile environment. The court reporter was set up, ready to begin, and looking bored. The lead attorney, Charlotte Adams, was sitting back, making some notes.

"Good evening, Charlotte," he said, approaching her.

"Evening, Bryson," she replied, and didn't engage in further small talk. He took the hint when she looked back down at her laptop.

He took a seat at the end of the table and picked up the packet that was already laid out for him. Listed were the questions Cam would be asking Misty. As Bryson scanned quickly through them, another knot of tension formed in his stomach.

Tonight wasn't going to be pleasant. Looking at his watch, he noted that it was a bit past four. They'd be lucky to get out of there by seven. And the hours that this took were going to be draining on Misty. He wished he could somehow take the pain on himself — not make her relive her time with Jesse Marcus.

At the sound of murmuring outside the room, Bryson looked up in anticipation. "Ridiculous," he muttered.

"What was that?" Camden walked through the door with a smirk on his face.

Damn, Bryson felt like wiping that look off. All thoughts vanished, though, when Misty stepped through the doorway behind Cam, tucking a strand of her dark hair behind her ear.

With the barely heard click of the door shutting, they were all closed in. Bryson usually would have found the room a bit claustrophobic, but he wasn't thinking in those terms right then. He could do nothing but devour Misty with his eyes.

He ignored Cam's taunt and stood up, thinking she was just about the loveliest creature he'd ever laid eyes upon. Very little makeup adorned her high cheekbones, and her sparkling green eyes nearly had him drooling. Her hair cascaded over her shoulders and hung free down her back, leaving images in his mind of her sitting atop him, her breasts peeking out through those glorious dark strands.

He was instantly hard as a rock. If he hadn't sat back down immediately, he'd have gained a reputation as an unprofessional pervert. But he couldn't help himself. One look at her and he was ready to demand that everyone exit the room so he could lay her out on the table and relieve this pressure that had been building inside him from the moment he'd tackled her in that crappy fast-food joint.

This woman was going to drag him with her to hell. It wasn't a matter of *if* anymore. They were going to be together; there was no stopping it. He just didn't know how far it was going to go — what the endgame would be. He knew beyond a doubt that they'd make fireworks happen when they came together. He just wondered whether once would be enough.

Somehow he doubted it.

His expression must have been predatory, because when she glanced up and met his eyes, her own grew large as she seemed to be caught by him, and then her chest heaved as if she couldn't get her breath. Yes, they would certainly make fireworks happen.

"Sorry about your hard time getting here, Bryson," Camden told him. "I hope everything worked out okay for you. Misty and I took the time to go over the process so she could be ready when we came in. Charlotte has agreed to let me ask the questions so Misty might feel more comfortable." He led Misty to her seat and then sat down across from her. "We should get started right away, though, since we're already running so late."

"I apologize. After I spoke with another witness, my flight got delayed," Bryson said, glad his voice came out clearly. No traces of weakness to be heard.

"Misty, we're going to jump right into this because it could take a while," Camden warned her.

"That's fine," she replied. She was obviously nervous, but she still sported a determined set to her shoulders.

Bryson felt a deep urge to jump up, to tell Misty she didn't have to go through this — that they had enough witnesses, and they'd just keep her in protective custody until the trial ended. She'd been so afraid, so on edge, and although she was standing strong now, he suddenly didn't want to hear this, not after what Cam had said, not after knowing something about how bad her life had been.

He had to protect her. Everything inside him screamed to do just that. But before he was able to make a fool of himself and say any of this, Camden asked the first question, and as he waited for her reply, he was grateful he'd kept silent.

"Can you tell us when and how you met Mr. Jesse Marcus?" Camden asked.

Misty took a deep breath. "I was working for a mini-mart gas and food store when he arrived at about three in the morning and came to the counter for cigarettes. I looked up and there he was in his uniform, and he began flirting with me. He seemed so charming, and I was taken in immediately." She spoke with embarrassment, but she continued. "The next night he came back and asked me on a date. I said yes."

Though her voice started out quiet, as if she was ashamed of her stupidity, as she continued, her shoulders firmed, and a determined glint shone in her eyes. This might be therapeutic for her, might help her to realize she had nothing to fear now.

At least that's what Bryson hoped.

"Was he still in uniform when he asked you on a date?"

"Yes. He was on shift. I got off at four in the morning then, and the third night he came back, meeting me at the end of my shift. I didn't own a car then, but I lived a little less than a mile away, so I walked — I know, I know — but he offered me a ride home. I was so impressed that this officer wanted to take me home, keep me safe, so I took the ride. I thought, what could be safer than getting a ride home with a cop?" She shuddered. "So he took me home. He had a flower in the car for me. I was even more impressed. Jesse is a big guy, and at first, he seemed incredibly good-looking, leaving me to wonder what he saw in me."

"So, Jesse dropped you off and then left?" Camden prodded her.

Misty sighed as she squirmed in her seat. "No. When we arrived at the apartment, he parked in the back of the building, where no one came in or out. I thought it a bit unusual, but then I realized he probably wasn't supposed to give civilians rides, so I wasn't concerned, assuming that he was protecting his job." She stopped speaking, and it was obvious she was reluctant to continue.

"Please go on," Camden prompted gently.

"I thanked him for the ride, and I reached for the car handle to get out. He grabbed me. He said there was no rush. I should have been afraid, but I was with a cop," she said, her eyes a bit wide. "So we sat there and talked for a couple of hours. I heard traffic begin to pick up as the morning commuters left for work, and then he grabbed my arm and pulled me against him and kissed me. I was so awed that this successful, handsome policeman wanted me enough to kiss me, I didn't think about the fact that he wasn't giving me a choice — that he'd just grabbed me and taken the kiss almost forcefully. Then, he got a little…'handsy.' His fingers tugged on my shirt as I squirmed to get away. At this point, I wasn't comfortable anymore and didn't want him touching me, but I wasn't sure how to pull away. It all just happened so fast. When I was starting to get frightened, his radio went off and he had to leave. That was the end of our first date, I guess you'd call it."

"What do you mean by *handsy*? Did he try to force himself upon you? You said he was grabbing at your shirt, but did he push it further? Please don't hold anything back out of embarrassment," Camden told her.

"No. He didn't force me down or anything; he was just very…aggressive — I guess that would be the word to use. We were kissing, and his hands…wandered beneath my shirt, over my…uh…breasts." Misty's cheeks turned scarlet, and she shifted, lifted her water glass, and took a long sip before going on. "I was in no way ready to have sex in a car with a virtual stranger, but I now know that if the radio hadn't buzzed, he would have pushed it to that point. He was reaching into my pants. I thought at the time that he was just worked up, that he would have stopped…"

"This isn't your fault, Misty," Camden assured her. "You are the victim."

"Thank you."

"When did you next see Jesse Marcus?" Camden asked immediately. It was better to press forward.

"The next night, I was off work. There was a knock on my door, which always alarmed me because I didn't live in the best part of town. When I looked through the peephole, I saw that it was Jesse in his uniform. I was a little surprised that he knew which unit was mine, because he hadn't walked me to my door, and it's a large complex. Then I remembered he was a cop and it wouldn't be difficult for him to find my place. I opened the door and he came inside. As he looked down at me, that was when I felt the first stirrings of fear. What was he doing there? But I was still feeling a mixture of fear and excitement." She fidgeted in her seat.

"So, was he still working if he was wearing his uniform?" Camden asked.

"Yes. He said he wasn't off the clock for a few more hours and he'd like to take me to breakfast when he was off."

"Did he leave after that?" Camden knew the answers, but it needed it all to be on record.

"No. He sat down at the table and told me to come over to him. I was scared but still excited. He was a cop, one of the good guys, and he was giving me attention," she said with disgust. "I walked over to him and he pulled me down onto his lap. His belt pressed against me, but before I could think about being uncomfortable, or think about how strange the situation was, he was kissing me again. Jesse was a very forceful kisser. He didn't even give me time to breathe. His hands were once again wandering all over and I could barely get enough oxygen, but I was overwhelmed. I thought he was so aggressive because he was excited about me," she practically whispered.

"Please go on," Camden said when she paused.

"When he yanked off my shirt, I asked him to stop, but he laughed, as if he thought that was real amusing. It all happened so fast. One minute I was on his lap, the next, he was carrying me to the couch. I told him to stop a few times, but he ignored my words."

"I know this is hard, but I need you to continue."

"He...uh...we had sex," she sighed. "It was over really quickly. He didn't even undress, just pushed his pants partway down. When he was finished, he sat on the couch and pulled me into his arms, cradling my head against his chest. He told me it was all okay, that everything was fine. We were going to be real good together, that I was perfect. He said he'd be back in a couple of hours for breakfast. Then he left. I was so stunned, I didn't know what to think. He was a cop. Had I done something wrong? Had I encouraged it? I was so confused. I showered and put on layers of clothes and then waited. He showed up and took me out to eat, acting as if nothing was wrong. I thought I had to be the one in the wrong at that point."

Misty glanced over at Bryson and saw the unadulterated fury in his eyes. This wasn't easy for him to listen to. She had a feeling that if Jesse were in the room with them right then, the man would find a bullet in his head. She turned away from Bryson's intense gaze and focused on the table in front of her. It was either that or she'd never be able to finish her story. It only got worse from here.

"I don't know how it happened, but within a week, he took over my life. He moved me into his place even though I tried to protest. It was like a whirlwind. One minute, I was on my own, and then the next I couldn't do anything without his permission. The first time he hit me was when I told him I didn't want to leave my apartment. I only got a black eye from that exchange. It was one of the least painful punishments," she said, hanging her head.

"Can you tell us a little about your childhood? The jury needs to understand you, understand why he was able to bully you." There was no judgment in Camden's voice.

"I was an orphan. My mother dropped me off at a fire station when I was a baby. The only things that were with me was a dirty old T-shirt and a note that said to contact my brother, Damien, when I got old enough. I don't know how that note stayed with me through the years, but somehow it did. Not that I was able to ever contact him. I wouldn't know where to start, even if the person ever really existed. No last name, you know. I was bounced around a lot, and life wasn't easy, but that's not an excuse..."

Misty didn't see the way both Camden and Bryson tensed at her words. This wasn't something Camden had asked earlier. This wasn't something she told people often. For one thing, she didn't think the brother really existed. For another, whom would she tell? She had no ties to anyone.

"You have a brother?" Bryson asked, interrupting the deposition and getting a stern look from Charlotte Adams.

"I don't know. That's just what the note said," she answered, looking at him with wide eyes, wondering what she'd said that suddenly had both men so uneasy.

Bryson was glued to his seat as he began putting puzzle pieces together. He'd loved her eyes, the beautiful green color, the shape, everything about them, but something about them had bugged him from the beginning, almost as if he'd seen them before.

Now, he knew. He knew a Damien. It couldn't be possible, of course, that this was the same man she was speaking of. The world didn't rotate that way, didn't connect like that, did it?

"Not now, Bryson," Camden warned him. "Let's continue, Misty. Tell me what happened next."

Misty spoke for a while longer, telling about her time with Jesse. Her eyes filled with tears a few times, but she kept her emotions in check and spoke almost like a robot.

"...and then I couldn't take anymore. I went to the police and filed a report after he punched me so hard that one side of my face swelled. It nearly left me blind in one eye. I tried to leave him," she choked out.

"Did the police help you?" Camden asked.

Misty laughed, a chilling sound that dropped the temperature in the room by at least several degrees. "Jesse found me at the hospital. He took me away from there, his eyes colder than I'd ever seen before. No one tried to stop him. He told me he was going to show me exactly what happened to women who betrayed him." Her voice was frightened, as if she were reliving that horrific moment in her life.

"He handcuffed me and forced me into the back of his car, then drove home to the apartment and marched me up the stairs. My head still hurt from the last beating he'd given me. People watched him take me in. No one said a word to stop him. I was so frightened, I didn't even try to resist — I knew it would only make it worse. As soon as we were inside the apartment, he forced me to my knees, my hands still handcuffed behind my back. I had to perform…I…he…thrust himself into my mouth, pushing so hard I threw up a little, and somehow my lip was cut and throbbing. I begged him to stop when I could speak… I couldn't even breathe… But he just laughed. I could see how much he was enjoying it. When I thought it was all over, he pulled me to my feet and took me to the bedroom… He undid the cuffs long enough to remove my clothes, then he cuffed me to the bed. The torment lasted for two days. He took turns raping and beating me." Misty's voice came out in a monotone as she forced herself to withdraw, to think of that time as a movie, not her own life. If she pretended she was speaking of some other person, maybe it wouldn't hurt so much.

"This needs to stop," Bryson demanded, his eyes glittering with rage.

"I know it's difficult, Bryson, but if you can't handle it, you have to leave the room. We need to do this." Camden shot Bryson a dark look.

Bryson looked as if he was going to come out of his chair and throttle his friend. The two had a stare-down and Bryson wasn't backing off.

"I'm fine, Bryson. I promise," Misty said. The last thing she wanted was to see a fistfight start.

He didn't look pleased, but he sat still, arms crossed, as he waited for her to continue.

"I didn't really know how much time had passed. I went in and out of consciousness. It wasn't till it was over that I realized it had been two days. He never let me up from the bed. I was lying in my own…urine…"

The shame was there for them to see, making it even harder for Bryson to listen to her talk of such humiliation. He wanted to kill Jesse with his bare hands for doing this to her.

"He broke three ribs, fractured my jaw, and I had an infection in my wrists. When I did finally get to the hospital, I lied, said I was kidnapped, but got away. He told me that if I gave any other story, the next time I wouldn't be alive to tell another soul."

"Were you in fear for your life?" Camden asked.

"Definitely. He told me of his last girlfriend. He told me she would never be found. He said there were several 'bitches' who would never be found, because they'd been stupid enough to betray him. He said the only reason I was still alive was because he hadn't finished with me yet." A shudder passed through her. "He won't rest until I'm dead," she added, the words sounding so strange coming from her flat, almost expressionless voice.

"He won't ever get the chance," Bryson vowed.

She looked over at him again, seeing his bunched muscles, the harsh expression on his face, the quiet fury, and she was grateful. It was somehow calming for her, as if he were taking the emotions from her onto himself. It gave her the energy to go on, to keep telling her story.

"When I healed, I began planning my escape. I knew I had to sneak out; I knew I had to disappear. No one would help me. So I saved as much money as I could. It wasn't easy since he took all my paychecks and monitored everything I did. It took a long time, about nine months of waitressing, saving part of my tips, not all, or he would have known, but eventually I had enough and I bought a cheap car. I was ready to go, just a couple of days from escaping. That's when everything went horribly wrong. That's when I accidentally found a bunch of large bags of cocaine. He was furious with me. I don't know how I managed to get away, but I did. I escaped and was in hiding until Bryson found me."

Camden asked more questions, and she answered each and every one, and then it was over. Misty was done — emotionally and physically drained. She didn't know how she would manage to get up in front of a jury and say all of this again. It was one thing to speak in front of four people, but an entire courtroom? What if the cross-examination made her look like she was the bad person? She had stayed with the man, after all. Wouldn't they spin that into her being a willing participant in his depraved games?

"We're all finished, Misty. You've done very well." Camden moved his chair to sit in front of her while the court recorder packed up. "I know this wasn't easy, and I appreciate your strength in giving your testimony, but we can breathe a little easier now and try to put it all out of our minds. Easier said than done, I know, but how about we go get something to eat, maybe a stiff drink, and try to relax? You don't have to think about it anymore for now."

"I'm not hungry," she said, the thought of food making her stomach want to heave.

"You will be after about three or four straight shots," he told her with a smile.

"Would you like to come, Charlotte?" he asked, turning to the other woman, who they all seemed to have forgotten was even in the room.

"No. I appreciate your testimony, Ms. Elton. It will be valuable to the case. I'll contact Camden if I have follow-up questions," she said, and then was the first one out the door.

"She's scary. I'm glad you're the attorney helping me," Misty said as she looked at the open door.

"Ah, she's a sweetheart, but this case has everyone acting unusual. There's just too much that can go wrong," Camden said. "Now, let your attorney buy you a meal."

"I guess…"

"Good. Let's get out of this room," Bryson said. He almost shoved Camden aside, then leaned down and pulled Misty gently from her chair. "You are braver than I could have ever imagined. I'm so sorry you had to go through that."

It didn't take much for Misty to fall against his chest and accept the comfort he was offering.

"I was a fool, but I didn't know how to get away," she said, ashamed of herself for once again leaning on a man — even if this man seemed to be one of the good guys. She'd made that mistake before, but maybe, just maybe…

"Look, you were a victim and Jesse abused his power as a cop, abused it, and you, horrifically," Bryson countered.

"I just want to forget about it," she said.

"Then let's go."

Bryson wrapped his arm around her shoulder and led her outside, with Camden following quietly. Misty looked up to the clear night sky and let the stars calm her. She was safe now. Though she was closer to where Jesse lived than she'd been in over a year, she felt safe. He couldn't get her.

Or at least she felt like he couldn't. Not with Bryson there next to her.

CHAPTER NINE

MISTY SAT IN the backseat of the SUV and listened to Bryson and Camden shoot the breeze as they drove from Camden's offices to a small country bar and grill. She was glad they weren't expecting her to talk, because she didn't think she'd be capable of it right then.

The experience had drained her. It was so much harder than she'd imagined to lay this story out on the table again. She'd learned Jesse's character only too well while living with him, but after talking about it, voicing what he'd done to her, how many times he'd violated her, and in how many ways, she had no idea how she'd survived as long as she had.

No matter how despicable the person, Misty never delighted in the end of anyone's life, or even by the idea of it, but she had to admit that if Jesse were to die, she'd sleep a lot better at night. Sure, she felt guilty, but she wouldn't take the thought back. She considered him the incarnation of evil, and, yeah, she wished him dead.

She felt raw and exposed as she huddled against the leather seat during the ride down the dark road. The two men had chosen a restaurant outside town; was it so she could have time to collect herself? She doubted it would come to them as a big surprise if she had a complete breakdown.

But Misty was stronger than they gave her credit for. No, they hadn't put her down or made her feel like a weak woman, but she knew her eyes were hollow, knew her body was shaky, knew the signs of a meltdown were all there. But Jesse hadn't broken her down back then, and he certainly wasn't going to do it now. She'd had a will to survive. Somehow. And she still did. More now than ever before.

Would Bryson think differently of her now? Of course, that was almost a stupid question, because she really had no clue what he'd thought of her before she'd told her ugly tale. She knew she was developing feelings for him, but wasn't it more of a white-knight complex? He was there to save her, a quintessential damsel in distress, from the evil dragon. When this was over, one way or another, she was sure these strange feelings would go away — this need for him to be nearby would evaporate.

If Misty had felt nothing for Bryson — no attraction, no thoughts, no...lust — then she could have dealt with the situation far more easily. And anyway, because she was so torn up, so ragged, so raw, could she trust her feelings at all? Maybe she was attracted to him because that was easier to handle than thinking about her ex and the horrendous things he'd done to her.

Maybe she was projecting her emotions. And getting them

all muddled up.

What would it be like to be in a relationship with a man like Bryson? Did he just seem like a white knight now, but when he got close to a woman, did he turn into a monster? How did two people find each other and live happily together? She knew those existed — they had to, or why would babies still be born? Why would anyone marry? There had to be happy endings out there. Maybe she just wasn't one of the lucky ones.

She hadn't even been given a family, the one thing she wanted more than anything else. No. Instead, she got to walk this world alone. That had to be why she was having fantasies about a life with Bryson. He was the first man ever to be kind to her. Still, it was his job; it wasn't about her at all.

Bryson had it all already. A family. Friends he loved and respected. For all she knew, he could have someone special in his life now. Maybe the way their eyes connected was just a part of his job. It made more sense than that he might actually be attracted to her. Because, having it all, Bryson certainly didn't need her.

Their lives were just so different. If he disappeared tomorrow, there would be a manhunt for him. He would be missed by his family, by his friends, by the ones he protected. That was something that would never happen with her. She had disappeared for an entire year, and Bryson had come looking for her only because he needed her to testify. If she hadn't been mixed up with Jesse, she could have walked off into the night without a single soul the wiser. A single soul who gave a damn.

Of course, if she hadn't known Jesse, she wouldn't have

needed to disappear. But then again, where had her life been going? Nowhere. She was working a dead-end job, living in a ghastly apartment, and she had no friends, no purpose.

How long until she just naturally faded away on her own? Anger filled her as these thoughts flitted through her mind. Okay, so she'd been abandoned as a baby, but that didn't make her worthless. Everybody deserved a chance to shine. Perhaps she just hadn't found her moment yet.

"Are you doing all right back there?" Bryson asked.

She blinked, and it took a moment to realize he was speaking to her. Her emotions were already whirling, and the gentle tone of his voice, the concern in his shadowed eyes as he looked back at her, made it even worse. She'd given her deposition. Why did he even care how she was feeling? It made no sense.

Just as the attraction she felt toward him made no sense.

When she finally spoke — "I'm fine" — her voice came out scratchy, raw, exposed, just like her, as she struggled to subdue the violent tears threatening to erupt.

He twisted around in his seat, then reached back and carefully laid his hand on her knee, squeezing gently. "We're almost there. I should have sat in the back with you."

"No. I promise, I'm all right." She wanted him to stop before she gave in and let out the full explosion brewing inside her.

His eyes told her he didn't believe her, but at least he released her knee and turned forward again. She slumped against the backseat and closed her eyes as she took in several deep, cleansing breaths.

If she wasn't careful, she'd think she was falling in love with this stranger. Logically, she knew it couldn't be real. She didn't know him, and he certainly didn't know her, or know anything about her beyond what she'd said today. And that wasn't pretty.

She tried to be smart, tried to explain to herself what she was feeling, but it was beyond her. All she could wonder was this: what was she doing even thinking that another man was attractive, especially after reliving her past with Jesse? Surely most women would never contemplate entering another relationship after the trauma she'd been through. But most women weren't as lonely as she'd been most of her life.

And most guys didn't show as much compassion as Bryson had shown toward her. It was all for the testimony, she forced herself to remember — or was it? Sometimes it seemed like more. It seemed as if he actually cared. But that was foolish, wasn't it?

The SUV stopped, and Misty quickly tucked away her thoughts, telling herself that everything was fine, that this had been a hard day. Now they were going to enjoy a friendly meal, and then she'd go to her room and sleep.

The next day, they'd head back home, and that was the last she'd see of Bryson until the trial. There was no way she was going to analyze how much that thought bothered her.

If she never saw Bryson again, she would never experience his lips against hers. She despised herself for it, but it seemed almost the only thing on her mind of late. When she recalled how his eyes had blazed in anger over what Jesse had done to her, she found herself wanting to wrap her arms around Bryson, wanting to thank him, wanting to feel his kiss. She knew it wasn't about his touch — just the idea of a man's touch terrified her — but it was about a connection, about actually feeling something other than fear when in the presence of a man. And Bryson inspired no fear, except maybe of her bizarre feelings for him.

Her door opened and there he was standing in front of her, looking so incredibly handsome. "Madam," he said with a flourish, and after a moment, she smiled shyly, his over-the-top goofy grin driving away the dark thoughts she'd been having.

She was stunned into silence by his sudden flirtatiousness. Her eyes surveyed the scene, noting that Camden was leaning against the car, not saying a word. Wasn't Bryson's behavior a little unprofessional? Her emotions were so raw, she didn't know what to do, so she sat there dumbfounded.

When the silence dragged on, his teasing expression vanished; he held out a hand and said in a more even tone. "Please, may I escort you to dinner?"

"Thank you," she murmured, taking his hand and stepping down from the SUV.

Just his touch sent fire zinging through her veins. She was out of control right now, and she didn't know how to rein herself back in. Her only salvation was that he couldn't hear her thoughts, didn't know what was going on in her head, or realize that her heart was pounding as he gripped her hand.

Misty knew she should tug her fingers away, but they felt so warm and secure tucked against Bryson's that she couldn't.

She was in deeper trouble than she'd realized. She wasn't just falling for this guy; she was falling hard. When she finally hit the ground, she'd be lucky not to shatter into a million pieces.

They walked through the front doors, and Misty was immediately charmed. Though the building hadn't looked large from the outside, it was surprisingly roomy once they stepped through the doors, and it sported log furniture and red-and-white checked tablecloths. Various rodeo pictures hung on the wall, along with several signed photographs from country music stars. A band was setting up on the stage.

"A lot of musicians come through here," Camden said. "Some of them well-known. It's a local secret."

"How can you keep it a secret if it's someone famous?"

"Because the people of the town treat the bands like neighbors instead of celebrities, and they get to play a gig at a place like one they may have started at. We get a treat of great music, and they get to be regular guys and gals for the day. They never say when they're coming, and our people never leak it out once they're here."

"That's pretty neat. I'd never have thought this the type of place to attract a big musician. I mean, it's nice, of course." She didn't want to put his choice of bar down. "It's just kind of small and out of the way."

"That's what makes it so great," Bryson jumped in. He'd been coming to the place for years.

"Hi, Camden," said a woman as she approached. "You picked a great night to come in."

"Hey, Alyssa. Can we get my favorite table tonight?"

"Of course you can. If someone was there, I'd just make them move." She threw him a flirtatious smile, then turned toward Bryson and Misty. "It's been a while, Bryson," she said, stepping right up and throwing her arms around him.

"Sorry about that, Alyssa," he told her, genuine affection shining in his eyes.

"Well, just don't let it happen again. You go and get all busy with the FBI and forget all about us in the backwoods."

"If I recall correctly, Alyssa, you had a hankering for the big-city life, doing cover shoots all over the world," he countered.

"Yeah, yeah, that went real well."

"You did great. I found that cover from your fitness magazine, and no one has ever done that rag such justice."

"It was short-lived, but I sure grew up." Something had obviously happened to hurt her during that time.

"Some people never get to live — just remember that," Camden said, his words hitting Misty like a loaded shotgun. "But we're being rude. This is a friend." He paused, making sure to get her name right. "Magnolia."

Misty was taken aback when Alyssa gave her a hug. "Any friend of the boys is a friend of mine," the woman said with a genuine smile.

"It's great to meet you," Misty replied, her throat suddenly tight. How would it feel to make friends so easily, to have a real friend to share with? She feared she'd never know.

"We need to quit standing in the doorway gabbing," Alyssa said, and she led the way to a nice corner table in the back of the room.

Misty noticed only about six other people in the place.

"The special is Doc's meat loaf and loaded mashed potatoes with a heaping side of grilled asparagus," Alyssa said as she started to write on her pad. After the men ordered, she looked at Misty and waited.

"Um, that sounds good." There was no way Misty could eat that much food, but the guys had automatically chosen the special, and her leftovers would be good the next day, and possibly the day after that.

"Do you like your drinks virgin or with a bite?" Alyssa asked Misty.

"Um…with a bite," she said hesitantly, expecting to get a list of choices.

"I'll bring out your salads and drinks," Alyssa said instead, and then left.

"We didn't order drinks," Misty said to the guys.

"Sorry, darling," Bryson said. "We're both so used to coming here. Alyssa knows our drinks. Plus, first-timers always get a free special drink. You'll love it."

Misty shrugged, though the use of an endearment dropping so easily from his tongue made her tingle a bit. "When in Rome…"

Alyssa brought out the drinks and the boys were right — hers was exceptional. It had a tangy, zestful flavor, and before she knew it, the first one was gone and another one was in its place. Within half an hour, her worries were pushed back to the farthest reaches of her mind, and she was laughing softly as Camden and Bryson told old "war stories" about the bar.

"Did you grow up here, too, Bryson?" she asked, her eyes slightly droopy, but her body relaxed. She munched happily on her dinner salad.

"Yes. Born and raised." He tipped an imaginary cowboy hat.

"Is your family here?"

"Yep. You know about my little sister. She is hell on wheels, literally. She races dirt bikes, and gives me a heart attack every single time she goes on one of those tracks. The stunts she pulls — *criminy*. I don't think I'll live to be an old man."

Misty loved that he was an overprotective big brother. What would her life have been had she been raised with a brother? That is, if Damien really existed other than as a name scribbled on a piece of paper.

"And then I have an older brother. He's a good man, the fire chief here, actually. He's done it all, including firefighting in NYC. He finally got sick of the big city and came home a few years ago. My mom and dad, who still live here, were happy to get one of their kids home. I'm in and out, but gone a lot for work. They keep hoping I'll eventually take a field office job and stay here. I haven't found a reason to yet," he said, and then looked into her eyes.

Was he saying she could be a reason? It had to be the alcohol buzz in her head, because there was no way a man would change his plans for her. She just wasn't the type of woman for whom men would jump through hoops. If only…

"Then there's my grandmother," Bryson said with a groan.

"Is she okay?" Misty asked, making both Camden and Bryson laugh. "I don't get it."

"Sorry. You'd have to meet the woman. She's in her late sixties, I think. Well, I can't get anyone to tell me her actual age, but whatever age she is, it hasn't slowed her down even the tiniest bit. The poor sheriff has even had to arrest her and her best friend, Bethel, for disturbing the peace."

"Really?" Misty really, *really* wanted to meet this woman.

"Yes, really," Camden said. "The poor sheriff is seventy now, and he gave both ladies a stern lecture, but they didn't care. They're recapturing their youth or something."

"Yeah, I was surprised Cam's dad wasn't with them as a partner in crime. The three are pretty close," Bryson added.

"Your grandma and his dad?" Misty was more confused.

"Yeah, my dad is older," Cam said, "and Bryson's grandma had his mom when she was quite young, so they're close in age."

"Oh, I wasn't saying anything bad…"

"Don't worry. We didn't take it that way," Camden reassured her.

"Do your parents get upset when things like that happen? The arrest, I mean." Misty found it so nice to sit back and hear about their families. Jealousy was sitting there with her, but not the ugly kind. She just wondered what it would have been like to have her own stories like this to tell.

"Hell, no," Bryson replied. "They think it's great that grandma is having fun. The more she lives life, the longer she'll be in this world. I wouldn't be surprised if my parents join the terrible trio in a few years."

"I think the sheriff will definitely retire if that happens," Camden told them.

"Considering he would never be able to draw his weapon in a shootout, that may be his wisest choice," Bryson said.

"Yeah, I don't think Big Blue — his gun — has been shot in over twenty years," Cam said.

"I'm sure there are cobwebs in the barrel, maybe even a few spiders' nests."

The men continued to banter back and forth until there

was a tapping noise from the microphone. Then someone spoke. "Good evening, everyone. I hope you don't mind if I play a few songs."

The fork stopped halfway to Misty's mouth, and her eyes nearly popped out of her head once she turned and looked up at the stage. Her heart was pounding.

"Uh, Mis…Magnolia, are you okay?"

She heard the words through a tunnel. This couldn't be happening. Things like this didn't happen to her. *Not her*. This kind of thing was for lucky people.

"Are you choking, honey?" Alyssa was patting her back.

"F…fi…fine," Misty managed to stutter.

"Aw, don't worry, boys. She's just a bit starstruck. It happens to the best of us." Alyssa laughed and walked away.

Misty barely heard her.

She also didn't notice the tilting of Bryson's eyes as he gazed at her, not entirely amused at her complete absorption with the stage.

"*I can make anybody pretty…*" Brad Paisley began singing his hit song "Alcohol," and Misty didn't hear another word from her male companions. She was fully focused on Paisley as he ran smoothly through a couple of songs. Alyssa set down Misty's meal, and it went untouched.

When Brad jumped into "Two People Fell in Love," Misty sighed. All the trauma from her deposition earlier in the day was forgotten as she drank in one of her all-time favorite singers. When he began a guitar solo, she just leaned back and enjoyed.

"Thanks, all. I'm going to try that meat loaf now," Brad

called out through the microphone, then hopped down from the stage, and Misty's eyes grew round as he made his way to their table.

"Hi, Camden, Bryson. It's been a while." The singer pulled out a chair and turned it around before he sat, leaning against the back of it.

"Yes, it has been. It's good to see you. How are the wife and kids?" Camden asked, after they all shook hands.

"Kim and the boys are great. I'm on my way home tonight and had to stop in here. This tour is kicking my ass. I'm definitely missing the family."

"Yeah, I wouldn't know how that is, since I don't have any rug rats waking me at six in the morning," Camden said with a laugh. "Oh, this is our friend, Magnolia."

"Good to meet you, Magnolia. You have a beautiful name," Brad said, sticking out his hand.

She didn't know how she did it, but her arm magically lifted and then her fingers were encased in his. "H…hi," she managed to say without too much of a stutter. She was sitting at the same table with Brad Paisley! She'd just been introduced to him! They'd shaken hands! And everyone was treating it as if it were no big deal.

"Here's your food, Brad," Alyssa said, and she handed him a bag.

"Thanks, gorgeous." The star took the bag and then stood. "Hope to see you boys again soon. You keep promising to come out in the summer."

"Hey, the invite goes both ways, Brad." Bryson said.

"Aw, hell, Bryson, your daddy just wants me down here so

his ornery horse can buck me off again."

"Coward," Camden said with a laugh.

"Yeah, yeah. I'll talk to you soon."

And then Misty just sat and stared as he walked from the room. She could now die and say she'd lived her dreams.

"Are you still in there, sweetie?" Alyssa asked with a knowing laugh.

"I…wow," Misty said.

"Don't worry, darling. I had the same reaction the first dozen times Brad and a few others walked through those doors. Now, I'm used to it. What you have to remember is they're just like you and me," she said before pausing. "Okay, maybe not just like us. He does have one killer ass."

"Thanks, Alyssa," Bryson practically growled. The last thing he wanted Misty thinking about was another man's ass.

"No problem, sugar," she said with a wink. "Here are some boxes for your leftovers, which looks like Misty's entire meal. I don't think I ate at all the night Blake Shelton came in. I actually cried when he got married."

"Aren't you just so helpful," Bryson said with a glare.

"I do what I can," she told him before sashaying away.

"Are you ready?" Camden asked, a persistent smirk attached to his face.

Without another word, Misty stood up, gathered her belongings and moved toward the door. This night had been… fun. She hadn't expected to enjoy herself, hadn't expected to have a good time. She'd assumed that she'd just be sitting there listening to the two friends talk.

Not having fun didn't bother her — it was the story of her

life. And when she didn't expect anything good, her hopes were never dashed.

But she had ended up having one of the best nights of her life. Oh, who was she fooling? Certainly not herself. It had been *the* best night of her life. She floated back to the car.

The drive back to the hotel was punctuated with very little conversation. Camden turned on the radio and she sat back and absorbed the lyrics. Music had always been a solace for her, a way to sink into another world. She could pretend she was the woman the singer was speaking so fondly about, or she was the hero who got to win the day. She could be anyone she wanted to be through music or books.

It was an escape — a desperately needed escape.

When they arrived at the hotel, she clambered out of the SUV quickly before Bryson could open her door for her. She'd be able to take the gentlemanly thing for only so long before she ended up in a heap at his feet. He walked her silently to her door.

She took out her key card. "You don't need to walk me here. I'm fine."

"I just want to make sure the room is all clear," he said, giving her barely nine inches of personal space.

"No one knows where I am," she said as the door opened.

He stepped inside. "Better safe than sorry."

"But you're going to make Camden wait. Aren't you going back to his place?"

"No. I'm staying right next door." His words gave her all sorts of new butterflies. They were going to be only a wall apart. Eeek!

"All clear," she said, her voice high.

"Yes, it is," he agreed, suddenly far too close, his body heat seeming to radiate right on up to her and then begin a low-pressure tornado, growing hotter and hotter each time it swirled around her form.

Oh, my, he smelled good. The only men's cologne she could recall before this night was Jesse's, and it had made her gag. Whatever Bryson was wearing was spicy and woodsy and pure male.

"I should leave now," he said, but he leaned just a little closer.

Oh, she wanted the kiss, wanted to close the distance between them more than she wanted her next breath — more than she wanted to wake up the next morning.

What were they talking about again? Misty was at a complete loss. "Yes…it's…been a…uh…nice night."

"You are testing every good intention I've ever had," Bryson told her as he cupped her cheek in the palm of his large hand.

She didn't know what he meant by that and she certainly couldn't speak and ask him to clarify. They stood motionless for several drawn-out seconds, just looking into each other's eyes. It was the most intimate moment she'd ever had, and she felt things building inside her that she couldn't even describe.

"This case needs to end," he muttered. He released her face and took a step back, then a few more.

Without another word, he walked out through her door, securely shutting it behind him. Misty staggered a couple of steps backward, then sagged onto her bed, thankful it was there to catch her. Seeing the covers beneath her brought to reality how close a bed had been to the two of them while Bryson had been looking deep into her eyes. Would she have protested if he'd leaned in and kissed her, if he had lifted his hands and...?

She doubted it. And that was more frightening than any other thought she'd had the whole evening.

CHAPTER TEN

A FULL NIGHT in bed did the body good. At least that's what Bryson was desperately trying to convince himself of. And so what if he'd barely slept? A full day lay ahead of him, and he had a job to do. Today, the job was to get Misty back to her temporary home in California, and then he had a desk full of paperwork that his supervisor had piled on with glee.

With the way things were progressing, the case would be ready for trial soon. Jesse Marcus would be behind bars, and Misty would be truly safe for the first time in…well, maybe since the moment she was left at that fire station.

Once this was all over, the two of them could both go back to their regular lives.

The biggest problem with that was that he couldn't quit thinking about her — couldn't stop fantasizing was more like it. He'd been in charge of plenty of witnesses before, several of them beautiful and single, women who had thrown a lot of signals his way.

He'd never been tempted to risk his job over any of them, tempted to risk his own ethics. There was a reason agents didn't sleep with witnesses. It tainted their testimony. What if they suddenly said the agent was bribing them? What if it ruined their character? No lustful deed ever went unpunished. Besides, it just wasn't right to have sex with them. Each one was there to be protected, not taken advantage of, even if they were the ones pushing for a romp in the bedroom.

Misty was different, though, he tried to tell himself. But, then again, isn't that what all the people who crossed the line used as rationalization? She was special. It was meaningful. Gah. He was driving himself insane.

Maybe it was because he felt some alien emotional connection to her. It had to be a need to fix her broken heart. No, he didn't mean *heart*. He meant her broken spirit. Yes, that was it; it was just a desire to fix her. Damn! He was now spouting poetry in his own head. This was ridiculous.

Yes, he wanted to protect her, and yes, he wanted to mend her shattered heart, her shattered soul, but it wasn't because she was just anyone. It wasn't because she was his job.

The bottom line was that he was just making excuses to himself to feel less guilty when… no…*if* he took her to bed.

Nonsense. He was a special agent, a professional. He wasn't tempted at all.

He was also a moron, because of course he was tempted. What he really wanted to do was peel her clothes away, touch her the way a woman should be touched. Not with intent to hurt, not with a desire to overpower, but with compassion and passion — with a need to please.

So tempted.

"Get a clue," Bryson said to the mirror as he looked at himself in disgust.

"And now I'm talking to myself. Maybe I should see a shrink."

He shook his head and frowned. He was beginning not even to recognize himself. He'd never before felt so on edge, so out of control.

Walking from the motel room, he leaned up against the railing on the front balcony and waited for Misty to emerge from her room. He was early, but he hadn't wanted there to be any chance of her having to wait for him. He knew she wouldn't knock on his door. Besides, he was eager to go home. He had a few things he needed to check on.

There was a lot to do and he'd feel safer once she was tucked back into her place in California. It was guarded — not as heavily as he'd like, but a U.S. marshal went by — and he'd insisted that Axel go in about half an hour before their return to ensure that no malefactor had forced an entry while they were gone.

Axel had laughed at him, telling him that either he was becoming paranoid in his old age, or that he was so far over the edge for this woman that he might as well give it up now and haul her to a preacher.

Axel was wrong. He couldn't fall for a woman this fast. It was just infatuation. It was like being a child at the candy shop, and *really* wanting the red sucker, but your mother wouldn't let you have it. That's all this was — Misty was the red lollipop.

Okay, and he was the sucker.

When her door opened, she stepped out wearing a pair of leggings and tugging at a red sweater. Nothing fancy, but those clothes made his mouth go dry. Because she was in them. It didn't matter what she wore. She looked astounding in anything, whether it was a skirt and blouse, or jeans and a T-shirt. He wouldn't mind seeing what she looked like with nothing on at all. Then he could make a more accurate judgment.

No. He couldn't be thinking that kind of thought right now.

"Morning," he drawled, taking satisfaction when she jumped and spun around.

It wasn't fear in her eyes. It was worry, the same worry he felt. At least they were both confused by this growing attraction between the two of them.

"You startled me," she said, lifting her hand to her chest and rubbing.

Great! Now his eyes were focused on the luscious curves the sweater wasn't doing much to hide. As if sensing that what she was doing was only making the situation more strained, she immediately dropped her hand.

"Sorry about that, Misty." For startling her, or for staring at her? He didn't know what he was sorry for. For everything, probably. "Are you all ready to go?" He moved away from the railing and snatched up the one bag she'd brought with her.

"Yes. I can get that," she said, but he grabbed it anyway.

Why did a woman make it so damned difficult for a man to carry her bags? His father would beat him blind if he stepped around the corner and saw Bryson's hands empty while she was lugging a suitcase, even if it was a small one.

The two of them walked slowly down the steps to the parking lot, where a car was waiting to take them to the airport. During the drive, both of them were silent. Bryson didn't know what she was feeling, but he was uptight and anxious, ready to explode if he didn't get something figured out soon, and he thought it best if he just kept his mouth shut. When his phone rang, he was more than grateful to take the call instead of sitting there inhaling her scent with thoughts of pulling her across his lap.

With the way he was behaving, he wasn't that much better than her abusive ex right now. Bryson had worked too long and was far too professional to act this way. If he didn't get himself under control, he would have no choice but to resign from this case — and that was something he'd never before had to do.

He was still on the phone when they arrived at the airport, but he ended the call and collected her suitcase. There was a delay on their flight, and when they finally got on the plane, they ended up sitting in separate rows, her in front of him. As irritated as Bryson was about that, he thought it might actually be better for all concerned, considering the mood he was in.

Leaning back against his seat, he was surprised to feel his eyes grow heavy. He didn't sleep on planes, not usually, anyway.

CHAPTER ELEVEN

SOMEHOW SHE'D DONE something to upset Bryson. That could be the only explanation for why he hadn't spoken more than two words to her since they'd left Montana. She just couldn't figure out what was wrong — or, more specifically, what *she'd* done wrong.

Maybe he was disgusted with her now. First, he'd had to listen to her testimony about Jesse and the things she'd allowed that vile man to do to her, and then she'd ogled Brad Paisley. She'd be disgusted with herself if she weren't still starstruck. But it would explain why Bryson wasn't speaking to her.

Up to this point he'd been so kind, so charming, so comforting, but she'd long realized that it was probably all part of his job — keep the witness happy, secure, and ready to testify.

She was too chicken to ask him what was going on, so she simply matched his silence when they landed, while she walked by his side as Bryson grabbed her carry-on bag, and when she kept pace with him as they left the airport and were transported to the parking lot. A whole lot of silence.

In just a little while, she'd be all alone back at her house, where she could break down and have a good cry if she wanted, or maybe throw on some sweats and go for a jog. She couldn't figure out at the moment which she'd prefer.

Probably the jog, since it would burn more calories than tears would. Besides, she'd been too sedentary lately, and a jog would tucker her out. True, she might well pass out in the first five minutes because it had been so long since she'd run. For a short time during her year with Jesse she'd been on a fitness quest, and that was probably the only reason she'd been able to make it to her car and escape him.

He'd allowed her to jog only in certain locations and only while he was there to ensure that she didn't speak to any other men, but she'd been happy with the activity. It had given her a few moments of peace. He'd liked the result of her being in such great shape — her body was able to take more of his abuse.

The thought of running outside among so many strangers was a bit daunting, but she wasn't going to let her old fears — heck, her new fears, her constant fears — hold her back. She'd already made that decision and she was sticking to it.

If she chickened out on the very first activity she decided upon after giving her deposition, she was once again letting Jesse win. So, yes, a jog it was, she thought emphatically. Exercise saved lives.

She and Bryson arrived at her house and she didn't even try to argue when he insisted on walking her inside. This time, though, he brought his briefcase with him, and she wondered what he had planned. With the silent treatment he'd been giving her, she figured he'd want to be in and out of there as quickly as possible.

Once he'd checked all the rooms, he moved to her kitchen table and set down the briefcase. "I know you're tired, Misty, but I want you to look at some stills taken from surveillance footage. If you can identify any of the people with Jesse in these photos, that would help us. I know you won't remember dates, but if you can tell us if these people were ever inside Jesse's apartment and if you saw anything, we can strengthen the case even more."

She didn't really want to continue diving back into that world, but how could she say no? The more help she gave, the more chance this would all end. Maybe sooner than everyone hoped.

"Why didn't you have me do this sooner?"

"Because we wanted your testimony first, so it was from you alone, and not from something we'd placed in front of you, planted in your brain. The prosecuting attorney will look for anything to weaken our case, and if he thinks we in any way tried to persuade you of anything, lead you to any conclusion, he can make the jury believe that. We have to do each of these steps in a certain order."

"I understand," she said, though she didn't really. None of this made a lot of sense to her; at least the process behind it all didn't. What she did fully understand is there was a possibility of Jesse's going to prison, and if he did, he could never touch her again.

"Drink this," he said, placing a cup of water in front of her.

Without thought, she gripped it and sipped as she began flipping through the hundreds of images. Then her world tilted, taking her back to that hellhole of an apartment. When she saw him going up the stairs with a small, dark-haired girl, the picture dated a few months after Misty had left, she felt sympathy for the woman.

"I wonder if she's still alive," Misty whispered, and Bryson leaned over the back of her chair to see which picture she was looking at.

"No. Sadly, she isn't alive. Though he took up with her after you, I'm hoping that maybe you will have some information on her. Did you ever see her around?"

More fear shot through her. She could have been this woman, one of the ones whom Jesse killed when he was done with her. Every day she was thankful to have escaped.

"I don't remember her. There were several women, as you know, that he brought in while we were still together, but her face isn't one I remember. And I don't think I would forget. I don't think I'll forget a single thing from that time in my life."

"No, I don't think you will, either. I only hope that over time, you will start to heal, and eventually it will all be nothing but a vague recollection, without any measurable sting." Bryson laid a gentle hand on her shoulder.

She focused back on the picture. "She's so pretty here. Why does he do this? Why does it make him feel like a man? I just can't understand it," she said. She'd received broken bones, been raped, violated, and chained — and she'd been one of the lucky ones. How could this man get away with so much, ruin so many lives?

"She was loved by her parents, and missed greatly. I don't know why he does what he does, but he won't ever touch you again, Misty. That time is over — it's in the past. If we didn't have to dredge up the past, making you go through this day after day, you'd be so much closer to healing. I'm so sorry." Bryson took his other hand and clutched her other shoulder, letting her know he was right there.

Needing the contact, needing some sort of connection, Misty placed her fingers over his. She was closer to tears at this moment than she'd been while giving a detailed account of her own torture. Seeing another victim made it all so much more real.

He hadn't stopped torturing women after Misty had gotten away. He would never stop. And he *would* eventually get her. She didn't know how or when, but he would. She'd tried to think otherwise, but she knew that now. Still, she'd made the right choice in giving her deposition, and she had no regrets.

"Come here," Bryson said, pulling her from the chair she felt glued to. Before she even thought of stopping him, he drew her against his hard chest, wrapping his strong, comforting arms around her back and holding her close.

She couldn't help but take what he was offering. There wasn't a price attached to this gift he was giving her. No expectations. He was just trying to make her feel as if there was another person in this huge universe who was with her, if only for this tiny moment in time. She allowed herself to feel something other than fear and sorrow, and she melted against him.

Sighing when his hands moved slowly up and down her

back, soothing, gentle, letting her know he was there to help — a friend, in fact — Misty found herself sinking further and further down a path she shouldn't take. But isn't that what she wanted? Didn't she need a friend? Still, how would she know? She'd never, ever had one.

There had never been anyone in her life she could lean on. No one to comfort her and make her feel better when life was at its darkest, no best friend to giggle with and tell her secrets to, no person to cry with when it felt as if the world were ending.

So, yes, she wanted a friend, but as Bryson's hands skimmed over her shoulders and ran gently through her hair, she knew it would also be nice to have more than a friend. It would be nice to feel his touch on her naked skin, to feel his lips slide across her mouth.

A sense of guilt for harboring such thoughts assailed her, but her desire was stronger. She hadn't thought she'd want a man again — not after what Jesse had done to her — but this was desire. It was more than desire. This emotion was unlike anything her body had felt before.

It didn't seem possible, but her body melded completely with his, and she had no idea where she ended and he began. If she just lifted her head from his chest, would he kiss her?

As she pushed against him in her desperation to get closer, she felt the clear evidence that he wasn't unaffected. But despite the way his arousal was pressing against her stomach, his movements remained gentle, his hands soothing. As her body heated further, her muscles tensed, and her mouth opened, he did nothing more than rub gently along her spine.

Would he ever kiss her? She was afraid to find out. Afraid that he would kiss her back — and afraid of the rejection when he didn't. If he could hear the thoughts running through her head, he'd know for sure that she had lost it, and he'd check her into a psych house.

But then he moved his hand to her neck, sending shivers through her, and his fingers grasped her chin.

He leaned back. "Misty," he whispered, sending instant heat to her core, a pulsing, molten heat nearly burning her from the inside.

"Yes," she said, not knowing whether she was saying yes to a kiss, or yes to her name.

He looked into her eyes for a moment longer before he groaned, then his head leaned forward and his beautiful lips took hers, making her knees sag as passion spiked to a boiling point in her hungry body.

One arm remained around her back, pressing her tightly against him as his other hand cradled her face and he deepened the kiss, his tongue sliding easily inside her willing mouth.

Their moans mingled as he caressed her lips, plundered her mouth, stoked her ever-building flames of desire. She didn't know how much time passed — seconds, minutes, hours. Time was irrelevant. As long as she was in the safety of his arms, she was unhurt. Untouchable, except by him.

When he pulled back, she grew confused and disoriented, and she felt as if her body belonged to someone else.

"I have to leave, Misty," he said, both hands on her arms, steadying her as she tried to clear the fog from her brain, tried to focus her eyes on his flushed face.

"What?" Her thoughts were muddled.

His eyes were on fire, and she could finally focus enough to see them.

"I have to leave now, or I'm going to lift you in my arms, carry you to your bed just a few yards away, and make love to you all night."

What was wrong with that? She didn't get a chance to ask. He groaned and looked away.

"You're a witness under my protection. I can't do this." He was speaking as if through pain.

Respect. That's what she was feeling — utter and total respect for this man. His job was important to him. She wouldn't be the person to interfere with that.

"Then you'd better go," she said, and he turned relieved eyes on her. Had he thought she was going to jump his bones? Well... No. She wasn't going to do that. Tempting, but no.

"I'll be back when I...uh...cool off," he said with a light chuckle.

"Better make it a while," she warned him. She needed some cooling off herself.

"What are you doing to me, Misty?"

He ran his hand along her cheek again. She turned her head and kissed his palm, unable to resist. She had to admit that she felt tremendous power when she saw a shudder run through him.

It was euphoric to feel desire, to feel burning need, and still feel trust, still know that this man wouldn't hurt her, wouldn't push her, would continue to respect her.

The more she knew him, the more her confused emotions

began to straighten out, and all she wanted was to call him back, hold him close, and take from him what he could give her. Security, respect, relief.

Without another word, he turned, seized his briefcase, and strode from her kitchen and out of the house. She heard his footsteps stop as he waited for her to lock the door, then he moved down the walk. She went to the window and watched him drive away.

She'd made that look of hunger enter his eyes. She turned that man on with nothing but a little kiss — and he'd been man enough to do the right thing and walk away. Right now, the right thing didn't feel very right, but she found herself smiling anyway, because she felt safe and protected. And she also felt desired. In a good way.

As she wandered to the bedroom and lay down, even though it was early in the afternoon, she wondered whether she'd been too hasty. Never before had her body ached so badly, and never had she needed someone so much.

And not just someone, but something. She wanted Bryson, but not just in her bed. She wanted his company and his comfort. She wanted him to hold her, to tell her she was safe. She wanted the man in so many ways, it was impossible to describe.

If she could just learn to trust herself again, then maybe she could believe what she was seeing, believe what she was feeling.

Instead sharing a bed with her usual companion, confusion, Misty drifted to sleep with a hopeful smile on her face. The jog would certainly be needed when she awoke, more now than ever before. She had a massive overload of hormones to burn from her body.

CHAPTER TWELVE

H E SHOULDN'T HAVE done it. He shouldn't have stolen a cup with Misty's saliva on it and had it tested for DNA. One of Damien's cousins had gotten a sample from Damien, and they both felt like spies in some cheap B movie, but they were trying not to get Damien's hopes up only to have him find out once again that someone he'd pinned his hopes on wasn't his sister.

His friend had gone through that four times already since the search had begun to find the baby his mother had willingly given up. Each time, Damien felt more and more sure that he would never meet his sister.

And, man, did Bryson feel guilty about Misty. Sure, he hadn't wanted her to suffer the same sort of disappointment as Damien had if he and Camden were wrong, and he tried to tell himself that he'd done the right thing, but he knew damn well that he hadn't. He should have spoken to her, treated her like an adult, not acted in such an underhand manner.

Yes, FBI agents lifted people's DNA all the time, but he'd never done so on someone he actually cared about.

The result was positive. Misty Elton was Damien Whitfield's missing sister.

So the news was good. But did the end justify the means? Bryson hoped she wouldn't hate him for going behind her back to find out who her family was.

When she'd mentioned the note and the name Damien, Bryson had thought the odds were firmly against his friend being her brother, and yet he knew that Damien Whitfield was searching for a lost sister... It certainly wasn't an impossible coincidence. That's when he looked at her eyes again, and he remembered where he'd seen similar eyes — Damien. They were identical in color and shape.

Eyes can lie, of course. But DNA is another matter. There was no doubt now that Damien and Misty were brother and sister. So he was holding a phone tightly against his ear, waiting. The ringing seemed to go on for hours, and his rug was surely going to get ruts in it because he couldn't stop pacing.

"This is Joseph!"

Bryson couldn't help but smile as the man's voice boomed through the telephone. No one would ever accuse the head of the Anderson family of being a quiet man. It didn't matter how much he aged — he would always be larger than life. And he'd most likely never die, either.

"Hello, Joseph, this is Bryson Winchester," he began, then wondered whether he'd be able to get another word in edgewise during their "conversation."

"Bryson, my boy! How are you? I figured you forgot how

to use a phone, it's been so long since you've rung me," Joseph scolded him.

"I'm sorry, sir." Bryson always felt like a disobedient child when Joseph spoke to him. Because he was friends with Joseph's sons, he'd been to the man's place a few times, and Joseph was certainly loud and a bit overbearing in his manner. But the man was also always very welcoming. It seemed incredible that he and his sweet and accommodating wife could make such a perfect couple. But they did.

"I suppose I can forgive you, Bryson. After all, you're a busy man. Have you found someone special yet? Last I spoke to your parents, they were heartbroken — simply devastated — that they still didn't have grandkids. They have three beautiful children, and not one of you has done the honorable thing — settling down and marrying, and giving them some nice babies to hold."

Damn. It was worse than just scolding. Less than a minute on the phone with this man and he felt as if he'd been pulled into the principal's office for skipping class or being caught under the bleachers with Suzy Summers.

"Work keeps me busy, sir. I see my family often, though."

"Well, I would hope so," Joseph said. "You've got good folks, Bryson, real good folks. Not everyone is as lucky as you are"

"Yes, sir. I'm well aware of that," he said, then rushed into his next sentence before Joseph could cut him off again. "I'm calling because I have news that I think you'll be excited about. It pertains to Damien, but I thought it would be best coming from you, since I don't know him very well."

"Go on then, and spit it out. I'm not getting any younger,"

Joseph bellowed.

A grin spread across Bryson's face. It wasn't a wonder at all that Joseph was loved so much. He could sure blow a bunch of smoke, but underneath it all, family was all that truly mattered to him. Not his billions, and not all that he'd accomplished — just having a beautiful, successful, happy family.

"I've found his sister."

Dead silence greeted his proclamation. Bryson was beginning to think he'd lost the connection when he heard a suspicious throat clearing.

"Are you sure, boy?" It almost didn't sound like Joseph anymore. His voice was unusually quiet and gruff. It sounded as if the large man was fighting tears.

"I had her DNA tested. I haven't told her about any of it yet. I didn't want to raise her hopes and then dash them if it turned out that Damien wasn't her brother. She's had a…difficult life."

"I hate to hear that," Joseph said. "It could have been so much better for her. I'll never understand why my uncle did what he did, why he had so much hatred in his heart." The story filled him with sadness even after all these years.

"What do you want me to do, sir? Should I wait to tell her?" Bryson had no idea what his next move should be. Misty was a witness in a case and had a dangerous man coming after her. But this was her family. They would be able to offer her more protection than he could. She'd been without them long enough.

"What's her name?" Joseph asked.

"Misty Elton. She's beautiful, smart, and strong — so strong. She's a witness in a case we're building against a dirty cop. She's been through hell and back, and she's fighting not to get sucked down there again. I *do not* want to see her hurt any more than she already has been. I don't know how she'll react to this, but I have a feeling she won't be averse to having a family. I just want to make sure it's what Damien really wants, because I'm sure she can't handle another rejection in her life. I won't let that happen," Bryson said, revealing more about himself than he should have to the meddling Joseph Anderson.

"I see," Joseph replied, all traces of tears now erased from his voice.

"I will let you digest this and then wait for your call," Bryson said.

"You won't be kept waiting long, Bryson. What you've done for our family shows what a great man you are. I'll happily welcome you into the fold."

What? Welcome him into the fold? Bryson wasn't calling about himself; he was calling about Misty. He had nothing to do with her family other than as a friend to the boys.

When he hung up the phone, he had no idea that his future was already mapped out in Joseph's head. The old man was shrewd and he'd just found another match.

And there was nothing that made Joseph Anderson happier than matching up his family members and seeing future generations brought into the world for him to rightfully spoil.

Although Bryson wasn't ready to tell Misty yet what he'd found out, he had to hear her voice, had to assure himself that she was hanging in there. It had been a few days since their return from Montana, and walking away from her had just about killed him.

He knew he'd made the right decision, but he still regretted leaving her that day. She'd wanted him as desperately as he'd wanted her, and he was beginning to think it wouldn't be so bad if the two of them spent some…uh…intimate time together. Yes, she was a witness, and, yes, he was responsible for her, but keeping each other warm on a cold night — what was so wrong with that?

Because it was against the rules.

Hell, the rules were meant to be broken.

He dialed her, and then he waited what felt like another eternity for her to pick up her phone.

Her *hello* came out breathless, and Bryson's groin instantly tightened. Criminy! First he felt like a disobedient child while speaking with Joseph, and now he felt like a creeper, getting a hard-on like a damn teenager from just the sound of her voice over the phone. What was his problem? He was in his mid-thirties!

"Hi, Misty," he said, his voice coming out deep and lustful. Yeah, that shouldn't frighten her. Why not cut straight to the heavy breathing?

She took a breath. "Hi, Bryson. What are you doing?"

"I just needed to speak to you," he said somewhat lamely.

"Is everything okay?" The instant fear in her voice sucked some of the magic of the moment right out of him. He couldn't imagine what it would be like to live the way she did — always afraid, always worried the next knock on her door or the next phone call was going to throw her into a life-and-death situation. And she had no one to turn to. No. That wasn't true — she had him now.

"Everything is fine. I just…I don't know. I just wanted to hear your voice."

"Oh," she sighed, and he didn't think she was unhappy to hear what he'd said.

"What are your plans tonight?" Why should he even ask? It wasn't as if he could just go over there, lift her in his arms and drag her into bed. Could he? No. No, he couldn't. He needed to stage an intervention, force his thoughts to permanently renounce the gutters they'd taken up residence in.

"Well, since I have the night off work, I have a smorgasbord of thrilling activities planned. While watching old romantic comedies, I'm going to attempt to make progress on that cross-stitch I bought, and then, if I feel real ambitious, I'm going to draw myself a nice warm bath and read the newest Dean Koontz book — because my life isn't scary enough on its own."

"Mmm, do you use bubbles or just clear water?" Now why in the hell had he focused on that *one* part of her sentence? Was he trying to cause himself more pain?

He was pleased and incredulous when she played along.

"I like lots of bubbles," she said, her voice low and throaty. "I stay in there so long, though, that they all begin popping and I don't have to rinse them away."

Hot damn! He found himself digging in his pockets for his keys and stepping toward his front door before he managed to stop himself. This was a very dangerous game they were playing, but he was too competitive to call a foul.

"I know a few places on a woman's back that are hard to reach. Need some help?" He didn't know how he wanted her to answer that question. But he knew how he needed her to answer it — needed her to answer so he could stay professional, that is. Because he was so close to saying to hell with ethics and to head right on over to wash her beautiful and surely silky back.

"I think I have it covered. I have one of those long-handled brushes," she said, but her breathing had deepened. Their little wordplay was affecting her as much as it was him.

"One word is all it will take, and I'll be at your door in less than ten minutes." Bryson wanted to kick himself for his weakness, but he was unable to take his offer back.

As he heard her breath whoosh in loudly on the other end of the line, his heart thundered. What would she decide? If he went there, he had no doubt they'd end up in her bed.

He'd worked long enough — early retirement was good, wasn't it? That's how badly he wanted her. Badly enough to risk the career he'd been building. Badly enough to throw it all away for one night with her.

Bryson somehow knew it wouldn't only be one night, though — he knew that once he sank inside her hot folds, he wouldn't be the same ever again. Even if he was thinking with his hormones, even though his brain was trying to put the brakes on, none of that mattered.

Logic wasn't possible in this situation.

He didn't know how long the silence stretched out, but he eventually heard a sigh, and his groin jumped.

"It wouldn't be wise, Bryson. There's just…too much in the way," she said, but he heard clear regret in her voice.

His body was going to be aching for another night, at least. Sure, he could talk her out of this — could change her mind.

If he showed up, he knew she'd let him in. But then she might hate him the next day and assign him to the same miserable category as Jesse. A night of pleasure wasn't worth that.

"Goodnight, Misty," he whispered, thinking it was time for a ten-mile jog. Maybe he'd just extend that to a marathon.

"Goodnight, Bryson."

He held the phone for several moments after she hung up, his fingers clasped so tightly around the device, it was a wonder it didn't break.

Finally he set it down, then went to his bedroom and changed. He was just going to run until he passed out. That seemed the only logical solution.

CHAPTER THIRTEEN

A CAR STOPPED outside her house, and Misty's knuckles turned white as she clutched the sides of the kitchen chair. Who would be out in this weather? She'd pulled the blinds down — storms made her even jumpier than she usually was — so when she heard footsteps outside her window, she had no idea who it might be. It couldn't be Bryson. He was gone, out of town. And though she knew it was silly, she felt vulnerable, unprotected.

The steps stopped and there was a knock on her door.

She was frozen to her seat, barely able to move.

This could be it. Why had she been so stupid? Her cell phone was sitting there useless, completely out of juice, and the storm had knocked out the landlines. She had no way of dialing emergency services — no way of asking for help.

Calm down. It was probably the guy down the street with the little dog. He'd come by once before to ask if she had dog food. He'd run out and wasn't going to make it to the store till the next day. Why would he have thought she'd have dog food when she didn't have a dog? Maybe this time, he needed some milk for his cats.

"Misty? Misty Elton?"

Her head snapped upward. It wasn't the guy down the street. And this wasn't an FBI agent or a U.S. marshal. They wouldn't have used her real name. With a thundering heart, she grabbed a large kitchen knife and approached the door. There was no more running — she was through with it.

* * *

"How in the hell did he get her address!" Bryson was nearly panicked as he yelled into his cellular phone. "No one has that authorization!"

"Listen, I'm just telling you what I know," Axel said, for once somewhat subdued. They'd been blindsided. "The man has connections. I don't know what else to say."

"Does she know yet?"

"Yeah, I'm afraid she does. She's been told."

"She must be a total wreck! I want to be there for her right this minute, but I'm at least an hour away," he shouted again, *almost* feeling bad about taking his mood out on Axel.

"Just get there," Axel told him.

"I will!" He hung up and pushed his car up to a hundred miles an hour. If something happened to Misty, it would be all his fault, and he would never forgive himself. Never!

Going as fast as he could in the storm that was brewing

from Misty's direction, he drove frantically down the dark freeway. Every mile he came closer to her, the wind picked up.

The road stretched on endlessly, and forty-five minutes later, his heart thundering, Bryson pulled up to Misty's house and jumped from his vehicle when it had barely come to a stop. After rushing up the walkway, he hesitated when he reached the door, listening for any sounds.

The power was out and he could see only the flicker of candlelight through the windows. Hearing no sound was more worrisome than if he'd heard something.

The curtain fluttered and he knew someone had peeked out at him. He waited, his body tense. How was she? What was her reaction?

His heart raced as he waited. It had been a week since he'd seen her last, a few days since he'd learned about her family. Then Joseph, it seemed, had decided he'd spent enough time not knowing her, and he wanted to call on her, needed to speak to her. Joseph hadn't even asked him first; the old man just rushed ahead, interfering — his characteristic modus operandi.

The door opened and Misty stood before him, her face pale, her eyes red from crying. This was worse than he'd thought.

"May I come in?" he asked warily, not sure what Joseph had told her — not sure if he was the last person she'd want to speak to again.

She opened the door wider without saying a word, and he stepped over the threshold, careful not to touch her yet. She looked fragile enough that one single movement might shatter her.

Following behind her as she walked into the kitchen and lit the burner on her stove top, he waited to see what she would say. At least the gas stove worked even during a power failure. It seemed to give her some form of reassurance to be doing something other than staring back at him in the semidarkness.

"This is a nasty storm," he said, needing to break the silence.

"Yes. I lost power a little over an hour ago. When you pulled up, I'd just gotten the candles all lit so I can see around the house, now that it's dark outside. Do you want tea? I need tea," she said, her voice devoid of emotion as she set the kettle on top of the flame.

"Sure. I'll have a cup." He didn't know what to say — this was a first for him. This woman had already been put through so much trauma, and she'd been all alone today when she'd found out the biggest news of her life. Because of him.

"What are you doing here?"

"I needed to see you."

"You didn't have to make the trip in this weather."

The kettle began to whistle and she removed it from the burner, then poured hot water over the tea bags.

"Yes I did." That was the truth. He'd needed to be with her all week. "I…I'm done trying to stay away."

She reached into the cupboard and pulled out cookies, then leaned against the counter and, picking up her cup, took a sip of the hot liquid. She seemed so close to breaking apart that he couldn't keep his distance any longer.

Moving next to her, he lifted a hand, placing it on her shoulder. "Tell me what happened." If she didn't trust him any longer, she wouldn't say a word. He held his breath.

"I…I have no one in my life…or, at least, I've never had anyone all my life. I don't…" She tried to gain control over her emotions. "I think you're the only person in the world I trust, Bryson. I…want to talk to you, but I shouldn't burden you." A tear escaped and rolled down her cheek.

He lifted his hand from her shoulder and ran his finger along the track that the tear had left, then cupped her cheek in his palm. His insides were twisted in knots as he watched her try to maintain control of herself. He wanted to take her agony away, bear the burden for her. "You can tell me anything, Misty. I want to listen. I want to be there for you."

"You know I grew up in the foster-care system, that I was bounced around and around and around. The only clue to my identity was one little note that was left with me, the note that said I needed to find my brother. I never followed up on it. What was the point? I'm sure there are millions of Damiens in the world, and I didn't even know a city for him, or a last name. I knew nothing." Her voice was clear, almost as if she'd rehearsed her lines.

She most likely had in the time she'd had to think since her visit with Joseph had ended. This is where he should tell her the truth, Bryson thought, tell her of his involvement in all of this. But he couldn't get the words past his throat. They just wouldn't come. He was too afraid she'd hate him, make him go away.

"Go on," he said instead.

"Tonight, when he showed up here, I was so frightened, afraid to answer the doorbell. But I made a promise to not run from anything anymore, so I didn't just ignore it. I faced it," she said, a gleam entering in her eyes during the last few words.

He broke in. "You are so strong and brave."

She went on without acknowledging his praise. "We just stood there facing each other in silence for a moment. I almost asked if Santa was in town. He was the largest man I've ever run into, but with the white hair and beard and practically sparkling eyes, I wasn't afraid. I was just in shock."

Bryson was too tense to say anything as she paused to take a breath.

"He tells me his name is Joseph Anderson, that he's my... cousin," she said with disbelief. "He couldn't be. He's too old, for one, and how would he know I exist, for two? Or that's what I thought until he explained it all to me. Apparently his uncle got involved with a much younger woman and then died, estranged from the family. They know my brother — Damien is real," she said with wonder.

"Are you going to meet your brother?" Bryson now caressed her hair, both to offer comfort and to fulfill his need to touch her.

"I'm scared," she admitted. "What if it all turns out to not be true? What if this is all just some sort of sick joke? What if this Damien is my brother but he hates me?"

"No one who meets you can hate you, Misty. I can guarantee that."

He couldn't take it anymore. He had to hold her. Removing the cup from her hand, he set it aside and wrapped her in his arms, her head leaning against his chest, his hands stroking her back.

"That's not true!" she sobbed. "My foster parents hated me, the other kids hated me, and Jesse really hated me."

"Oh, Misty, they were all fools. Don't you see that you were thrust into a life that wasn't supposed to be yours? You were supposed to have it all, a loving family, a beautiful life, with all the advantages in the world. Even though you didn't grow up with what you deserved, you have still managed to stay above water. So many would use a terrible childhood as an excuse to use drugs, or live a life of crime, but not you. Though times were hard, you trudged ahead."

"But I ended up with Jesse," she reminded him.

"Not by your choosing. He took all choice away, didn't give you options. He forced your hand, and even then you managed to escape. Not all his victims have managed to get away from him…alive."

She shuddered in his arms and took in deep breaths, trying to pull herself together. "I'm still afraid. Doesn't that make me weak? I'm afraid to take the hand Joseph is holding out to me. I'm afraid of meeting my brother." She paused before admitting what frightened her even more. "I'm afraid of letting you go right now."

She pressed her body more tightly against his.

He was the lowest and most disgusting of scum. She trusted him, was seeking comfort and reassurance from him, and his body was firing up, his brain focused on the curves pressed against him, his caressing hands well aware of her derrière only inches below them. He would burn in hell — and he'd deserve it.

"I need you, Bryson," she whispered, the words barely

audible. "Please."

His entire body snapped into action mode. Though he nearly shook in his attempt to do the right thing, he was hard in a second. But she was vulnerable, hurting, alone. He couldn't do this, couldn't make love to her right now.

It was wrong on so many levels, and there wasn't a punishment severe enough for him if he went through with this. She would hate him afterward. And she'd hate him even more when she found out he'd known about her brother and told her nothing.

He was trying to persuade himself to let her go, to lead her into the living room, where he could hold her until she felt better, when her hand slid across his backside, making him clench his teeth.

It looked as if hell was going to take him. Because there was no more turning back.

CHAPTER FOURTEEN

MISTY'S STOMACH WAS doing handsprings, her emotions were all over the place, and her whole world had been flipped upside down, but one thing was certain: being pressed up against Bryson, with his strong hands kneading the taut muscles up and down her back, felt so right.

Her anguish faded; the questions running through her head stopped. All she could feel, all she could think about, all she could concentrate on, was Bryson. She needed him to take this away — take away the choices, the decisions, the life-changing questions.

She needed him to take...her.

"Please, Bryson. Please touch me," she begged. She turned her head and leaned upward, her lips softly flitting across his solid jaw, satisfaction filling her when he trembled in her arms.

"You're vulnerable right now," Bryson argued, fighting to maintain control, but his rebellious hands moved down past the small of her back and gripped her luscious behind, pulling her tightly against his solid erection.

"That's why I need you. Too many people have hurt me... too many times. I can't remember sleeping one night — not a single night — where I felt safe, where I felt that, when I woke up, the world would be a little bit better. I just need this night. I need to be in your arms, and I need to feel what real pleasure is. Just once," she begged, her mouth now at his neck. She bit down gently on the skin before sucking it, wetting it with her tongue.

He knew this was it. Either he pulled away, took her into the living room and held her until she fell asleep, or he took her lips. There was no turning back if he did this. No way of redeeming himself. When she nipped his neck again, his mind shut off.

At least hell was warm...

"I have to have you," he groaned before one hand flew up her back and clasped the back of her head, tilting her face upward so he could bend down and taste her beautiful mouth.

Their lips crashed together like a wave hitting the shore, shattering any and all doubts that this could possibly be wrong.

He wanted her — there was no doubt about it, from the urgency of his mouth to the feel of his arousal pressing against her stomach, demanding to be freed from the tight confines of his clothes.

If she didn't have him, she would never make it through this storm; she would just float out to sea, never to be found again. She moved her arms up his body, wound them around his neck, and pressed even closer.

His tongue explored her mouth, sending sensations

through her unlike anything she'd ever known, and making her core tighten in anticipation.

She'd never felt any craving for sex, not even once. It had been something she was either forced to have or thought she had to have, but it had never been pleasurable. Yet from the way she was feeling now, she hadn't a single doubt that this would be earth-shattering. This would be what she'd dreamt about when she read a romance or watched a sappy movie.

This would be worth the buildup of the games they'd been playing for weeks, months.

If this was the only night the two of them had together, she wanted it to last. She knew she was pushing him, and she knew he'd regret it. He was too ethical and this broke the rules. But to hell with the rules. For this brief moment, she felt nothing but pleasure, and she deserved that — deserved to feel alive and free.

He broke away and she dragged oxygen inside her lungs while his mouth moved down the curve of her jaw, and then his teeth clamped on to the skin of her neck, causing a sting that he quickly soothed with his tongue.

"What are you doing to me?" he growled, passion and confusion in his voice. But his mouth traveled back to hers, and he took her lips again, accepting nothing less than her complete submission.

She could ask the same of him, ask for his surrender — but she already had it.

One minute she was fully clothed, and the next she wasn't. She'd been so focused on his mouth that she hadn't even noticed when he stripped off her slacks and her panties. But she noticed now, when his long fingers gripped her backside and he lifted her, spreading her thighs apart as he set her on the counter, slipped between her legs, and, still clothed, pressed his erection against her aching core.

"Oh, my," she groaned, her head falling back. "Too much…" It was all too much — the sensation, the feelings, the raw need.

"Do you want me to stop?"

Did she hear fear in his voice that she had changed her mind?

"Never!" she cried, and he immediately plundered her mouth again, capturing the moan rumbling through her as his hands squeezed the flesh of her bare behind.

"I can't get enough of you," he groaned. He trailed his tongue down her jaw, but this time he didn't stop. He let his hands move up her sides, then captured the top of her blouse and yanked. The material gave way easily, ripping apart and offering her panting chest to his mouth.

Tugging on her bra, he freed her breasts, and they spilled out, reaching for him. He didn't keep her waiting. His mouth found one nipple and suckled it to a pointed peak before he moved over and gave the same pleasure to the other one.

"More," she demanded.

Misty fell backward, her back held up only by the cupboards behind her while his mouth worshipped her breasts, leaving her even hungrier than before.

When he moved downward to her navel, she shook, but not in alarm at his clear intent. She needed more, and that's what he gave her. His mouth circled her wet heat and then his tongue was doing things to her she'd never dreamed of. She screamed when the first pulses slammed into her, then moaned long and deep as he sucked on her swollen bud, drawing out her pleasure in wave after wave of sensation.

Before she could gain her breath back, he was standing again, his mouth glistening with her pleasure, his eyes wild as he gazed at her, animal-like, hungry.

"You are even more beautiful than I imagined," he whispered, his voice raw with passion. "And I imagined being with you. I imagined it a lot."

"Take me, Bryson; take me right now."

It didn't seem possible, but his eyes grew even more feral and predatory as he reached down and freed himself. She felt an instant of disappointment that she didn't get to see him in all his glory before he was pressed against her. But he was now sliding inside her and any thought of disappointment vanished.

"Ohhh…" was all she got out before he began pumping his hips, a sublime pressure mounting within her as be began moving quickly in and out of her flesh, building an even more intense explosion inside her body.

All she could do was grip his arms and moan as she looked into his face, his eyes and their powerful heat shining back at her. He held her buttocks as he moved harder, faster, longer with each stroke.

When he leaned in and kissed her, his mouth almost frantic, his body quaking, she released again, crying out as this second round of pleasure seemed almost to tear her in half with its intensity.

With his own cry, Bryson pulled out and she felt hot liquid

spill out on her thighs, the sensation heating her all over again.

"I'm sorry," he gasped.

"I'm not," she said.

"No. I...I forgot to protect you. I'm sorry. I pulled out, though...I think in time," he said, his face against her neck.

She wasn't sure who was holding up whom.

"Oh" was her only reaction. That had been foolish, very foolish. It would be fine, though. He'd caught it, right?

"Let's get you cleaned up," he said. He moved away reluctantly, leaving her shivering on the counter and unable to move. She was too afraid her legs would fail her.

He quickly returned with a washcloth. Was this the end of their night? Would he now leave? The thought left her full of dread, but she'd done enough begging tonight.

If he wanted to go, she wouldn't stop him.

Neither of them spoke.

Then, so gently that her eyes stung with tears, he slid his hands beneath her legs and back, cradled her close, and began carrying her through the house. When he reached her room, he laid her on the bed, reached into his back pocket and set something on the nightstand, and then removed his clothes. Sliding beneath the covers, he pulled her into his arms and kissed her with aching sweetness.

"With the power out, it will take two of us to keep warm," he said, though a heater was the last thing she needed. Her body was on fire.

"Great thinking."

No more thoughts intervened, because he was kissing her again, taking his time now — they had all night, after all. He drew away her ragged shirt and kissed her stomach. He let his hands glide slowly up her bare back, and that's when he felt the light ridges there.

He froze for a moment, and then, after turning her on her stomach, he kissed along her spine. The candlelight didn't give him much of a view, but it cast enough of a glow to reveal scars from what looked like years of torture. He knew what she'd been through with Jesse — he just didn't know what she'd been through before that man. Her body was trying to tell him the story.

His heart ached as he kissed each scar he felt.

"Bryson?" She murmured his name as she tried to turn from his scrutiny. "Don't look at my back. It's grotesque," she said, her voice choked.

"It's beautiful, just like the rest of you, Misty," he replied, preventing her from twisting away as his fingers gently drifted across her skin. "You are so beautiful," he repeated over and over again until she stopped struggling against him, his lips and fingers just a whisper against her delicate skin.

If he did nothing else this night, he needed to show her how incredible she was — that the scars didn't detract from her exquisite beauty. Not one whit.

Seeing them made him only more protective of her, filled him with a greater need to make sure she was never hurt again.

Caressing her body — this time, he was unhurried — he got lost in her once again, for the rest of the stormy night.

CHAPTER FIFTEEN

"I SHOULD LET you get some sleep."

If humans could purr, that's exactly what Misty would have been doing, purring as she rubbed her paws against his impressively solid chest. Though his heart was beating easily now, it had been pounding half an hour earlier.

"I'm exhausted, and my body couldn't move if I wanted it to. But I can't seem to sleep," she murmured, fully relaxed, praying time would stop so she and Bryson could stay in this happy little bubble.

"Yeah, I know how you feel." His arm tightened around her and he pulled her even closer as he continued long, lazy strokes down the curve of her back.

"Tell me about your childhood. Was it good? Did you like having a brother and sister?" She was trying to be coy, but Bryson wasn't fooled. She was afraid to meet her brother. He was a complete stranger, though related to her by blood.

If Bryson could help ease her fears, he would.

"I love my family. Out where I'm from, it wasn't so unusual to grow up in a large family where everyone actually loved each other, but I've been around the world enough now to really appreciate what I've always had."

"I'm glad to hear that. It would break my heart if you didn't appreciate them."

Her words made him ache for her. He'd seen people in her situation many times over, but he'd never harbored such deep feelings for any of them. And that train of thought took any ideas of sleep away. Was he falling in love with this woman? He knew he was falling, but was it love?

He mulled that over in silence. Not only was he falling for her, and falling hard, but what really surprised him was that the realization aroused no fear. He'd heard people say that when a person found his or her other half, they just knew, and now he could understand what they were talking about.

Later. He would think more on this later. Right now, Misty was seeking reassurance, and she was looking for answers. He could do his best to give both to her.

"I was always close with my brother, who's older, but our lives have drifted apart these days, since we rarely get to see each other. One thing we both have in common is our little sister. I told you she's a dirt-bike racer. Well, it scares us both equally. Matter of fact, the last two times I've seen him is when we were at her races, making sure she was okay," he said with a chuckle.

"What would you do, jump in and catch her?"

"I would trade places with her in a heartbeat if she were injured, and, yes, I would jump onto the course and catch her if I could. Luckily, she hasn't had any terrible injuries. I know it sounds rotten, but I really hope she loses her passion for racing someday. I just…worry. I can't have anything happen to her."

"Does she get mad at you for interfering?"

"Yes and no. Only once did we have a big blowout fight about it. After that, I backed off…a little. And now she tolerates my nagging. She knows my concern is because I love her."

"If I were her, and you were trying to get me to stop, I would think it was because you didn't trust me," Misty interjected.

"Really?" he asked, as if the thought had never crossed his mind. "Of course I trust her," he said, as if any other option were ridiculous.

"Have you ever told her that?"

He was silent for a moment. "Well, I guess not."

Could it be that Bryson still had a lot to learn about family? Even Misty knew trust was important, and she'd grown up with no one. Maybe she'd learned that lesson the hard way: by not having anyone in her life whom she *could* trust.

"I think I'm going to have to see her soon," he said. Misty's words really seemed to have mattered to him.

That made all sorts of warm feelings flow through her.

His fingers came around and he started to rub the sides of her breasts, sending sweet sensations through her sated body. His touch evoked such incredible responses that she didn't think she would ever grow used to it. Maybe that was for the best. If she got too comfortable with it, it would hurt horrendously when it was gone.

"Should I meet Damien?" Here was the real question she'd

been wanting to ask.

Bryson was happy she trusted him enough to value his opinion. "I think you should go when you're ready."

"They want me to come right away. Joseph left me a ticket. Two, actually," she said shyly.

"Two?" he asked.

"Um, yeah. I told him about my situation. But he already knew!"

"I think Joseph Anderson knows more than most people," Bryson said.

"Well, right before he left, he said the tickets were open-ended. I could come as soon as tomorrow, or in a week if I wanted. I said that I didn't know if I could."

"What did he say?"

"He was real quiet for a minute, and then said that I had Anderson blood in me and the calling of my family would be too strong to ignore."

"Is he right?"

"I don't know. I liked him. It was odd. I've never trusted someone that quickly, but I just felt…comfortable during our conversation, as if I just knew he didn't want to hurt me. I don't normally feel that way."

"Yeah, I remember quite well that you don't take kindly to strangers. You Tased me," he said with a laugh.

"Sorry about that, Bryson."

"I'm not. I got to lie on top of you."

"That was an unusual first meeting…"

"So, Misty, do you want me to go with you?"

"I couldn't ask you to do that," she said, but he heard hope in her voice.

"I want to." He wouldn't push her, but he would be by her side, with or without an extra ticket.

He could tell she was undecided, so when she changed the subject, he didn't hesitate to follow her lead.

"What made you decide to join the FBI?"

He considered her question for a moment. "I was in the Mideast, fighting in the war, and I saw so many things that could have been done differently. I'm not saying anyone was necessarily right or wrong, but I saw things no one should see. When I came home, it was the same thing here. So many victims. I got recruited, and I never looked back. This is just where I fit, where I belong."

"Did you get wounded when you were fighting?" She hadn't seen any scars, but then again, they also hadn't had good lights — only the flickering candles.

"No. I was lucky. I lost some good friends, but I was never shot, or bombed. I have been shot once here in the States, though," he said matter-of-factly.

"Where?" she gasped. "How can you speak so casually about being shot?"

"It wasn't that big a deal." He seemed uncomfortable all of a sudden.

"Getting shot is always a big deal," she cried.

"I don't know why I said that, 'cause I *really* don't want to talk about it."

Misty was crushed. He didn't trust her. He didn't want to open up about something that was obviously traumatic for him. "I shouldn't have pushed," she mumbled, and she pulled back a little.

"Hey! Don't do that. It's not that I don't want to share. It's just...well...embarrassing," he finally admitted with a sigh.

"How could getting shot possibly be embarrassing?"

"I was shot in the ass," he said with a groan.

Misty was stunned. Was he making this up? Teasing her? Who would make something like that up, though? Should she just drop it? Suddenly she felt a giggle in her throat and she clamped her teeth down on her lip — hard — so her amusement wouldn't reveal itself.

"I can feel your chest shaking, you little wench," he said, flipping her so fast onto her back that she lost her grip on her lip and her laughter spilled out.

"I'm so sorry," she gasped. "I don't know what's wrong with me. Getting shot is so not funny," she said between fits of laughter. "But your tush seems to be accident-prone." She hadn't forgotten about the dog story.

"Don't worry; my colleague Axel, brother, sister, and everyone else I know has made a few butt jokes, or rather made me the butt of their jokes."

When she was just about to pass out from lack of oxygen, a new gleam crept into his eyes, and her laughter died away. Oh, that was a look she was beginning to know.

One second she was giggling uncontrollably, and then the next, he was hard and inside her. "Oh," she gasped. This was much better than laughter.

"I have ways of making you cooperate," he said, then lowered his mouth to hers and took her remaining breath away.

Yes, any thoughts of laughter had evaporated — moaning had taken its place.

CHAPTER SIXTEEN

T AKING A DEEP breath, Misty gazed out the windows, watching the clouds below her shifting, blowing, making shapes. Now a herd of elephants rushing to a water hole, now wild stallions roaming free.

Anything to take her mind off meeting her brother for the first time. This was forcing her to confront all sorts of emotions she'd never thought she'd have to. Her biggest fear? Rejection. As the plane made its final approach, her stomach dipped, her heart thudded, and the only thing holding her in place was the feel of Bryson's hand clasping hers.

What if her brother was cold, cruel, a person she wouldn't want to know? What if he had a great life and he was kind — too kind to reject the sister he wished he didn't have? Yes, she'd met Joseph, and, yes, he was a kind man, but this man, her brother, hadn't grown up with the Anderson family, either.

He'd essentially been an orphan, too. But look at him now. He was a mega-successful businessman with a beautiful wife and child. The most frightening part of all of this was how badly she wanted to know Damien — how badly she wanted him to love her.

How was it possible, through all the hurt she'd endured, for her to still want to be loved? It was ridiculous. Some would say she was simply setting herself up for failure. And they'd probably be right.

She looked down at the picture again and stared at eyes the exact same shape and color as hers. They both had dark hair; they both had the same smile. Shared genes were on full display here. She'd never expected to see anyone in the world who looked so much like her, but then she'd never thought she'd find him. Heck, she'd never truly believed in his existence.

But he was real. And she was about to meet him. Would the meeting help heal her, or would it shatter her ability ever to give her heart away?

"Breathe," Bryson whispered.

She hadn't realized she was now holding her breath. Bryson had been so good to her, understanding that she needed silence, that she needed to brood. He was another man she didn't deserve, but she was just selfish enough to hold on to him for as long as he would stand beside her — and all of her dysfunctional, irrational behavior.

It was strange to think that she had not only a brother, but a sister-in-law, too, along with about a million other relatives. And she was an aunt! Not that she'd want to meet the whole passel of them all at once. Not this first time — too much pressure. If, and it was a very big *if*, they invited her to come back, she could meet them gradually.

Right now, it would be too overwhelming. She wouldn't be able to enter the room — wouldn't be able to speak. What would they expect from her? Damien was hugely successful when they found him. If they thought she'd be the same, boy, were they going to be disappointed.

She was just Misty. She was nobody special. That was the most depressing thought of all. Yes, Bryson kept telling her that she was special, and he even made her feel that way, but for too many years she'd had people saying the opposite, saying she was a hopeless case, not adoptable, too many issues, too much work.

Ever since she turned three, after her first foster mother had passed the only people who'd taken the time to know her had been either those she was thrust upon, who at least got a paycheck to have her around, or those who wanted something from her — like Jesse.

Now she knew that she was related to the Andersons. Whoa! When she researched them, she'd become paralyzed with fear. Why would Joseph have bothered to show up on her doorstep? This man was loved and respected, and would probably win the next presidential election if he chose to run.

There wasn't a single good thing he hadn't done. His family had the golden touch — even Damien seemed to have inherited the Midas gene. Whatever they began always ended in success. And not just a little, but world-domination-style success.

Talk about intimidating.

Though she didn't want to think about it, she had to wonder what her life would have been like if she'd grown up with them, had cousins to play with, been able to attend the schools they did. If she'd had support from people who loved her.

"I can't do this," she whispered as the plane touched down and growled and vibrated during the jolting ride on the landing strip.

"You can, Misty. I know this family. They will love you, and you will love them. It will be as if you've been with them your entire life." Bryson turned her face toward his.

"But I'm a nobody, Bryson. They're rich and powerful, and they have each other. I'm an intruder, and Damien is probably horrified I exist, embarrassed that I'm showing up."

That would be the worst. If he looked at her with disgust, or pity, or coldness. If he looked through her instead of at her.

Pulling out the note from Damien's wife, she read her words again.

> *My dearest Misty,*
>
> *How excited I was to learn that a miracle was granted to us and you were found. We've searched for years, and it just goes to show that you were meant to be a part of our family. I know we mean nothing to you right now, and you're probably feeling confused, but please come and visit us — give us a chance to know you, and give yourself a chance to know us. I look forward to meeting you.*
>
> *Sierra*

Misty rubbed her thumb over the words again and again, some of the ink smeared from the tears she'd cried while reading it, tears she hadn't even noticed falling until she saw the blots on the fancy paper.

Sierra sounded like a lovely woman, at least from her letter, but that didn't mean that Damien wanted to know her. It only meant that he'd married someone fantastic. Misty was worried though, that Damien wouldn't want this. After all, his wife had been the one to write to Misty — the letter hadn't come from her brother.

She didn't want to be the source of anything negative, of problems between Damien and his wife. She'd caused others enough turmoil during her miserable life.

Existing in the streets and fighting for everything had taught her at a young age how to survive, but it hadn't shown her how to live, and it certainly hadn't taught her how to trust. So, here she was, about to meet her brother's larger-than-life family. What if she ended up throwing up on their expensive shoes?

That would certainly make a wonderful first impression.

As the plane pulled up to the gate, she felt her vision blur. This wasn't good.

"Misty!"

Bryson's voice was coming to her from far away. Maybe it was good. Maybe she would just sleep for a while. Then, when she woke up, this would all have been a dream. Her entire life would turn out to have been a dream, and she wasn't really an orphan, had never been with Jesse, and wasn't flying to meet American royalty.

But then, she also wouldn't have met Bryson…

CHAPTER SEVENTEEN

" ...ANXIETY ATTACK. HER eyes are fluttering. Ma'am, can you hear me? Can you open your eyes? That's good. Look at me. Good. Try to focus on me. No. Don't shut your eyes again. Magnolia, open your eyes!"

Magnolia? Who was Magnolia? They were shaking her as they spoke, but she didn't recognize the name. Who was this person?

Misty clawed her way through the dark tunnel, then wished she hadn't. A bright light was shining in her eyes, and several people were standing around her. What was going on?

Where was she?

Her heart began racing as she tried to catch her breath. Tried. She couldn't breathe.

"Get oxygen on her now!"

Something was placed over her mouth and her eyes shot open again as she reached up, clawing to get whatever was trying to suffocate her away from her mouth.

"It's okay, Magnolia," Bryson said. "The paramedics are trying to help you." His voice was tense but low as he tried to be reassuring. If he hadn't been panicked, it might have worked.

Oh, Magnolia! Her fake identity. So confusing on top of all the other confusion she was feeling. What if she messed this up? What if she made a mistake and then somehow Jesse found her because of it? They were in Seattle, though, weren't they? That was a long way away from him.

Not too far away, actually — only a single state. She was too rattled to think clearly.

She turned toward Bryson, caught his face in her vision, and was finally able to make her lungs work. He was her anchor in this tempest of uncertainties. He was what she would hold on to.

"That's good, ma'am," the paramedic said. "Don't try to talk. We're going to move you to the ambulance now."

Misty felt herself being lifted, and realized she was on some sort of board.

"I'm staying with her," she heard Bryson insist, and she hoped they allowed him to. They'd have to if they didn't want her passing out again. He was the only thing giving her some vestige of calm.

What had happened?

When they got her locked into the ambulance, she searched for Bryson again, and then he was there, stretching his hand out and taking hers.

"I'm so sorry, Magnolia. We pushed this too fast. We shouldn't have come here yet. This is too soon."

She wanted to answer him, but there was a mask over her mouth. Her frustration made her heart accelerate again, causing the monitors to emit loud beeps.

"You need to calm down, ma'am. We're only about five minutes from the ER now." The same paramedic as before was talking quietly and reassuringly to her.

He was good at his job, she thought. He had a soothing voice, and it helped.

The ambulance stopped and the back doors were thrust open.

As they wheeled her in, someone rattled off: "We have a twenty-nine year old female, appears to be an anxiety attack, no known medical conditions or allergies. She's suffering from shortness of breath and high blood pressure, and she's been conscious for thirteen minutes. Was unconscious for six minutes."

"Sir, can you fill these out?"

"Give them to me, but I'm staying with her," Bryson said, sticking resolutely by her side.

She was wheeled into a room, transferred to a bed, and then a doctor was taking her vital signs, checking her eyes, and calling out orders.

Words and phrases like *dehydrated*, *elevated heart rate*, and *low oxygen* were thrown out, but Misty ignored them, her eyes staying on Bryson. She would be fine if he remained with her.

Soon, she was hooked up to an I.V. and the room emptied; she was now alone with Bryson. After about fifteen minutes, her breathing became normal, her heart rate slowed, and she realized what had happened.

Angry tears stung her eyes. What a fool she was. She'd been so nervous over the visit, she hadn't eaten or drunk a thing in two days. She'd had trouble sleeping, and she'd been a mess. She couldn't meet her new family like this. How could they help but think she was too much work to bother with?

After an hour passed, the doctor came back in. "We would like to keep you here overnight, Ms. Linhart, just to make sure everything is under control. Our staff is going to move you to a room now," he said, then answered a few questions for Bryson.

Misty was silent as they moved her through the hospital. When she and Bryson were alone again, she looked over at him with worry and shame. "I don't have insurance. I can't pay for this."

How could she stay the night here? As it was, the cost of the ambulance ride and the ER would probably take her a couple of years to pay off. But to stay overnight would be impossible. She'd never clear up the debt.

Working part time for a retail store didn't give the best salary, and it certainly didn't offer her insurance. Trying not to panic any further, she took a calming breath.

"It's covered, Misty. Don't worry about it," Bryson told her as he took a seat next to her bed and handed her a cup filled with ice water. She didn't comprehend it at this point, but he knew that she was now part of a family who would never let her down. They would make sure only the best care was provided for her.

That was information for later, for when she was assured of her place in the Anderson family. Once she got to know them, she would understand that she would never be on her own again, at least as long as she didn't want to be.

"Please, I just want to go. I feel so stupid. It's my fault. I forgot to eat…or drink." Her admission earned her a semi-stern look. "I was so nervous…"

"I can guarantee you that your brother will love you. All the Andersons will love you. There is nothing for you to worry about," Bryson said.

But no matter what he said, she couldn't believe him. Heck, she was only coming to visit them, and she'd passed out. Was there nothing she could do right the first time around?

"He's correct, you know," they heard a male voice say.

Both of them turned to find Damien and Sierra in her doorway. How did they know she was there? What were they doing standing so close to her? She didn't want them to see her like this. It couldn't be the way she met her brother! What a nightmare…

"Yes, Bryson is right. We already love you. Now we just want to get to know you," Sierra said. Hand in hand, the two of them stepped into the room.

Misty was speechless. The newcomers walked over to her bed with a vase full of flowers and kind smiles on their faces.

"We should have come to you in California. I don't know what we were thinking. I'm so sorry, Mi…" He stopped and corrected himself. "Magnolia." He took the chair next to Bryson and sat down, then extended his hand, letting it be her choice to accept it or not.

Unsure what to do, she looked to Bryson, who gave her an encouraging smile. She turned back to Damien, who, to her shock, had tears in his eyes, and something more, something that looked like...hope.

"I've wanted to find you since the moment I knew you were alive, Misty. I was just a small boy when my mother told me the story about you, and I never thought I would know you, never thought I'd be able to find you. I am so thankful the day has finally come, though. I'm sorry — so truly sorry — for what you've been through. I feel fulfilled now because I finally have my sister."

She slowly accepted his hand, and he squeezed gently. He wasn't a monster. He wasn't unhappy to see her. It looked as if he really cared about her — a stranger. Yes, they were related by blood, but he didn't know her. Why would he care what happened to her? It was beyond her.

As if he could read her mind, he continued, "I know I'm a stranger to you, but I hope to change that. I hope that we can get to know each other, be a real family."

Misty looked into his kind green eyes and let herself cry. She'd fought it, but she couldn't any longer, and she shed a mixture of happy and sad tears, happy because this man she'd been so afraid to meet was far from a monster, and sad because she'd gone her whole life without knowing him.

No one could be such a great actor. And what would be the purpose? She had nothing to offer him. This had to be real. It had to be.

Sierra joined her husband's side. "I am so excited to have a sister. I want to learn everything about you." She beamed at Misty with eyes just as kind as her husband's. "I wrote you the letter because my husband started and stopped about a thousand times. We didn't want to frighten you away, but really wanted you to know that we couldn't be happier that you have been found. You're family."

"Thank you," Misty was finally able to say. It probably sounded lame, but no other words would come out. She was too choked with emotion.

"We don't expect you to do much talking," Damien said. "We were waiting for you to get off the flight, and when the ambulance showed up, I nearly had a heart attack and joined you in the back. We came right over, and I have a doctor here who's a friend, and he let me know where you were. I just couldn't rest until I knew you'd be okay. If you're up to it, then we'll just sit with you for a while." His words tumbled out as if from nervousness.

"I'd like that," Misty replied, her trembling body finally relaxing. Why had she been so anxious? There was nothing to be afraid of. Yes, they might not end up being the best of friends, but maybe they *would* grow close. Maybe she'd really found a family who would love her. And who would want all the love she was so willing to give away.

"Good. You are so beautiful, just beautiful," Sierra said. "Your eyes are the exact same as Damien's. It's amazing." She sported a wide grin on her face as she looked from Damien to Misty and back again.

Damien grinned too. "My eyes have always been my favorite feature. Now, I know why. I must have somehow known that they were a connection to you," he told Misty, making her practically glow.

"I've always liked the color of my eyes, too," she said, her cheeks flushing in embarrassment. She didn't normally like anything about herself — and on the rare occasion that she did, she never admitted it.

"It must be some sibling telepathy or something," Damien said, making Misty smile again.

"Thank you for inviting me here, for wanting to meet," Misty said. "It was a very nice plane ride."

"Well, until the part where she passed out," Bryson piped up.

"Yeah, that must have been hell on you, actually seeing it," Damien said, turning toward Bryson for the first time. "I'm sorry. I've been so focused on Misty that I've been rude. It's been a long time," he said, sticking out his hand.

"Yes, it has. It's good to see you, Damien."

"You, as well."

They all chatted for a while — maybe an hour. Misty didn't know. Time had ceased having any meaning, and she didn't want the night to end, even if she was stuck in a sterile room on a hard bed. Despite everything, she'd never had a more perfect night, not even when she met Brad Paisley; nor had she ever laughed so much. Her stomach was actually developing a cramp.

"Which room is it? Are you all incompetent? I have a relative to visit."

All heads turned as a loud voice echoed down the corridor and Damien jumped up. "I'd better save the nursing staff," he said with a chuckle. "Joseph, down here," he called out from the doorway.

"Well, there you are, boy," Joseph called back, and then Joseph was standing before her again. Oh, my. She'd forgotten in just a few days how intimidating he was, standing well over six feet tall with shoulders that seemed to stretch on forever. Luckily, the well-trimmed white beard and mustache softened his appearance. "I don't understand why it took so long for someone to call me. I was waiting for little Misty to arrive, and then I get a phone call saying she had an incident on the plane. It was like pulling teeth to get any information," he said, his voice lowering as he approached her bed.

"Joseph, she's Magnolia for now," Damien said with a meaningful look.

Joseph's tone quieted. "I'm sorry, Magnolia. I won't make that mistake again," he said, and he seemed honestly grieved over his mistake. Mistakes like that could cost everything they'd done to protect her.

"I'm fine," she said. All this fuss was beginning to make her uncomfortable.

"I'm sorry, darling. I didn't mean to scare you with all my bluster. I was just worried, that's all," he said as he scooted Bryson out of his chair and took a seat. Bryson laughed at the old man's antics.

"Everyone is fussing over nothing. I just…got dehydrated is all," Misty said, not wanting them to know she'd panicked at the thought of actually meeting her brother face-to-face. She was grateful when they let her get away with her half-truth.

"It's never nothing when you have to go to the hospital," Joseph told her, "but they will take real good care of you here. If not, they have to answer to me, and I'm not pleasant to deal with when I'm unhappy." He issued that warning just as the doctor walked into the room.

"I can vouch for that, Joseph," the man said.

Joseph chuckled and leaned back. "How's our girl doing?"

"Her vitals have improved greatly. She'll be ready to go home in the morning."

Everyone breathed a lot easier.

"It's good to see you still do a fine job here, Carson," Joseph said, and he stood up and patted the doctor on the back.

Misty's eyes were growing heavy, but she was afraid that if she went to sleep, they'd all disappear and she'd lose them forever. It would be so much more painful now that she'd had a taste of what having a family was all about.

"My patient is exhausted and clearly having a difficult time keeping awake," Dr. Carson said, "but I can see she's far too polite to say anything, so I'll say it. You head out and let her get some rest, and then you can pick her up first thing in the morning." The doctor's words earned him disappointed looks from both Joseph and Damien. But as they turned to look back at Misty, it was more than clear that the doctor was right.

"It's okay," Misty said weakly.

"We'll go and let her rest," Sierra interjected firmly. "Then we'll see you bright and early tomorrow." She leaned down and hugged her new sister-in-law.

"Fine," Damien conceded. Then he surprised Misty by also leaning down and pulling her into his arms for his own hug.

It took all she had not to cry again. She refused to, just refused to, until they left the room. After all, they'd seen enough of her crazy emotions for one day.

"Fine, I suppose," Joseph grumbled, then embraced her briefly but with surprising gentleness. "We'll bring you to the place tomorrow and take good care of you while you recover."

Then, just as quickly as they'd blown into the room, the three were gone, taking the doctor with them. Bryson also leaned down as if to leave, but she clutched his hand in hers like a vise to prevent him from going away, too.

He probably wanted to visit with the others, she thought, but she couldn't seem to command her hand to let his go.

She held herself together for longer than she thought she could, but when Bryson looked into her face and then rubbed his hand along her cheek, she began to unravel, her body shaking with the emotion she'd been trying to suppress.

"It's all right, hon. This meeting has been a long time coming. No one will think you're weak if you shed a few tears," he said, and that was all it took.

Her dry eyes prickled, and then she watched as Bryson's face blurred, and then the tears welled over and rushed down her cheeks.

"It's okay. Everything will be okay," he vowed. He slid into the bed next to her, careful of her I.V. as he pulled her gently into his arms.

Bryson held her close as she sobbed out her relief, as she let go of all the anxiety she'd been carrying. And as she let go of the last walls around her heart and let him in.

When sleep finally took her into its sweet embrace, she had nothing left to give — she'd let it all go and now the fate of her love was in Bryson's strong, capable hands. Meeting her family, knowing she belonged had opened her emotions up in ways nothing else could have.

Now, she was willing to hope, to dream, to want! She loved

Bryson; now she just needed to be brave enough to tell him. She tried to without the words, by holding him tight.

It was up to him if he wanted her love for more than a night or a week. She wanted him forever.

CHAPTER EIGHTEEN

Y OU'RE NOT GOING to have another anxiety attack
    on me, are you?" Bryson asked as they rode in the back
of the Jaguar that Joseph had sent to pick them up.

"I can't promise anything. Look at what we're being driven
in," she said with a nervous smile.

"I just want to give some warnings before you see the…
um…house." He was unsure whether the Anderson mansion,
with its high towers and stunning stone walls, could be called
a *house*

"I'm fine. They're just people, right? It's not like they weren't
born the same way I was. They are people. Okay, really *wealthy*
people, but people all the same. I can do this." Who was it she
was trying to convince — herself or Bryson?

"Yes, we are all born the same way," Bryson said with a
chuckle.

"It's ridiculous to be this nervous. I've already met them,"
she said, frustrated with herself.

"Just because they are affluent doesn't mean they're snobs. Just remember that they want to know you. They're excited about spending time with you, and they have a lot of love to give. I've known the family for a really long time, and I haven't seen a bad side to any of them," he assured her.

"So, why is this house so intimidating?"

"It's pretty much a castle. No, there's no *pretty much* about it. The place is a castle, but somehow Katherine has managed to make it warm and inviting, so don't think of your everyday dungeon kind of castle," he said with a smile.

"A castle — like a mote and all?"

"No, no mote. But there are high towers," he said.

"I guess seeing will be believing," she told him, and sat back as they covered the final mile of their journey.

When they pulled up the private driveway, and she got her first glimpse of the Anderson residence, her mouth dropped open. Bryson's description hadn't done the place justice, to put it mildly.

It towered above them all, looking far more suited to a hillside in England than a gentle slope in the state of Washington.

Wow! Just…wow!

The car stopped. When the driver got out, came around and opened Misty's door, she was so awed that she didn't even notice Bryson leaving the car. He magically appeared standing next to the driver, waiting for her to accept his hand and step out.

Her legs trembled when she finally managed to stand, and she was grateful that Bryson didn't let go of her. *They're just people*, she continued telling herself.

The huge front door opened and Damien walked outside.

"I would have come for you myself," he said as he stopped in front of her, "but I wanted to give you a little time on your own. I thought the drive would be relaxing."

He was far more perceptive than most men she'd known. But all she could manage to say was a rather shy thank-you.

"The entire family wanted to be here, but Katherine threatened them all if they showed up, because we have a *lot* of family and we didn't want to overwhelm you. It will just be a small event today. Well, not even an 'event.' Just know that you have many family members eager to meet you. If you're up to it, we can have them all gather tomorrow."

Misty didn't want to be rude, but she doubted she was ready for that. It was just too soon. Maybe if she and Damien got to know each other and it looked as if she'd be a part of his life, maybe then she could meet the rest of the clan.

"Can we...maybe...wait a little while?" She prayed he wasn't going to hate her now for her reluctance to get to know people he obviously loved.

"Yes, of course. I'm sure this is all insanely overwhelming." Damien's eyes were kind and understanding.

He shocked her when he stepped forward and pulled her close for a brotherly hug, her second from him. "I know I should hold off and not be too clingy, but I have wanted to know you for so long, and I'm so devastated that I haven't been able to always be there for you. I just want to be a big brother," he said, making her eyes sting.

She wanted to believe him so badly. Her arms slowly came

up and she hugged him back, something she hadn't been able to do the night before in the hospital. She fought furiously not to release her emotion. In the hospital she'd still been a little loopy. She was now fully alert, and this was probably the most important hug she'd ever received. She found herself not wanting it to stop.

"Okay, I'll back off now," Damien told her, and he released her from his embrace.

"I'm afraid."

"Of what?" he asked, reaching out a hand and taking hers.

"I'm afraid to love you and lose you. I've always known there was a possibility of your being real, but I've never been able to hold on to anything, and I'm scared that this is nothing but a dream."

Would he think she was a fool now? Should she have waited to express her fears?

"If you will allow me to be a part of your life, I'll never go away," he vowed. "That's not the way this family works."

She couldn't help but have real hope as she looked into his honest eyes.

But she was unable to break years of self-training. "Can we just take it a day at a time? I've found that's easiest."

"We will do it however it suits you best, Misty."

She smiled, with her heart pounding but the tautness of her nerves easing up as she read his expression. If nothing else, he was being sincere. If somehow this didn't all work out and have a happy ending, it wouldn't be because he wasn't trying.

"We have a special person we'd like you to meet today, though," Sierra said as she stepped outside to join them with a bundle in her arms.

Misty's eyes widened as she looked at the pink blanket. Her fingers shook as Sierra held the baby out to her.

As if she were taking hold of the most fragile and expensive antique, Misty was trembling as Sierra handed over her child.

"Her name is Samantha and she's two months today." Sierra shifted the blanket, and Misty looked down into the most precious little green eyes she'd ever seen.

"Oh, Sierra, she's perfect," Misty sighed.

Sierra beamed at Misty as she held her niece. "Yes, she looks so much like her daddy."

"And she'll be a knockout, considering there's a mixture of her mother's great beauty and her aunt's," Damien said with pride.

"Oooh," Misty gushed.

"Let's all go inside where it's just a little warmer," Damien said while Bryson stood at Misty's side and, looking down at the pink bundle, ran a finger across her soft little cheek.

"You should take her in case I trip," Misty said.

"You'll be fine," Damien assured her.

Misty didn't have as much faith in herself as everyone else did, but with Damien and Bryson walking beside her, she figured that if she did begin to trip, one of them would catch her and the baby. She was so focused on the baby in her arms that she didn't have time to be awed by the Anderson mansion's massive entrance.

They ended up in a sitting room, where she got to meet Katherine, a beautiful, petite, kind, gracious woman, who made her feel right at home. Joseph was there, of course, and he was just as wonderful as he'd been when she first met him, and in the hospital the night before.

Over the next few hours, Misty got to know more about the people she was related to, and she was finding that keeping her distance wouldn't to be an easy thing to do.

After only a few hours, she knew that to lose this family would be unbearable. Though she was used to loss, the hits came harder and hurt more as she grew older. Whatever it took, she decided, she would fight for this newfound family — fight for a happy ending for herself.

CHAPTER NINETEEN

S MALL WAVES LAPPED against the shore as the morning fog clung to the sand in an attempt to anchor itself. As it rose slowly in the sky, the sun was doing a decent job of winning the fight against the cold.

As Misty walked along the shoreline, looking down at her feet and making patterns with her toes, she let her mind wander. The night before had been filled with talking, laughter, and more information than she could process.

Her new family was vast — vaster than she would have ever imagined. What she couldn't understand was why her mother hadn't taken her to them if she was unable to care for her and Damien.

Wouldn't the two of them have had a much better life had they grown up where they'd belonged? Maybe her mother had simply been a selfish person. Misty had always had visions of her mother making the ultimate sacrifice for her daughter, doing what was best for Misty, or what she thought was best, by leaving her at the fire station.

Now, her reality was shifting. If her mom had really cared, she would have left her with family. It seemed now that her mom had only wanted revenge for her perceived hurts, and unfortunately, Misty had been the one to pay the price for her mother's sins. She wanted to ask Damien about the woman, since he'd at least had several years with her.

But once she opened that door to the past, it could never be closed again. It was like having a double-sided coin. No matter which way it landed, it would always be the same, and only one person could win. And that wasn't going to be Misty. She would learn the truth, but then she could never unlearn it. Was that what she really wanted? Wasn't it better to not have all the answers?

Though she couldn't find any fault with the company of the Andersons or her brother, she was enjoying the quiet calm of the sea at her feet, the solitude and peacefulness after a boisterous night.

Living in fear most of her life, she'd risen early for as long as she could remember. The last thing she'd wanted was to be caught unawares by some junkie while sleeping in an abandoned building. It was best to get up and keep moving, never let someone get a grasp on your routine, which meant she'd never developed a routine.

Her life certainly hadn't been boring.

A bit of monotony wouldn't be such a bad thing.

Her biggest fear now was that she just wouldn't fit in. How could she possibly be related to these people? Not only were they megawealthy, but they were also kind and humorous, and so accepting.

They were the exact opposite of her in so many ways. Even if Bryson thought she was a good person, enough other people had beat her down that what she believed about herself didn't measure up, and yet the Anderson family still wanted to know her, still wanted to accept her with open arms, her faults and all.

She had to admit that she was proud of herself, because she had managed to keep her insecurities at bay, and she'd managed to keep a smile on her face rather than looking like a goldfish flopping around after the cat had swiped it from the comforts of its little bowl.

Family amusements had zoomed around her, with Joseph and the boys smoking a cigar after the meal, telling stories, each one topping the other. The women, so comfortable with each other, spoke of activities they'd been involved in. Not once had the television clicked on; not once had there been silence. Her family members were comfortable in this amazing mansion, and though they had included her, she still felt as if she were on the other side of a glass wall, looking in. And yet she'd held it together, kept her anxiety from showing.

When it had come time for bed, she'd been disappointed when Bryson hadn't shared her room. Maybe he'd thought she needed time to absorb it all; maybe he needed a break. She wasn't sure of the reason, but she did know that she'd had plenty of alone time in her life, and she didn't relish the thought of a lot more of it.

But she couldn't allow herself to get too used to having him by her side. Yes, she was falling in love with him, but that didn't mean he felt the same about her. Most likely, once the case against Jesse ended, so would her relationship with this wonderful man.

As she continued walking, her thoughts returned to the Andersons, and she wondered whether she could mold herself into a woman worthy of being part of her family. Could she somehow change into a person who belonged? Other people managed to change their circumstances, change their lives. She *might* be able to do the same.

Maybe she could even be the kind of woman Bryson would consider forever with.

This absolute need to belong was painful. But it offered her a light at the end of the tunnel. Once again, it was hope that was her biggest weakness. Most of the people she'd known from her days on the streets knew their lives wouldn't improve, knew they were going to remain where they were for the rest of their lives.

They didn't bother with school or work. Society had given up on them, and so they gave up too. As much as Misty tried not to hope, she'd never been able to kill thoughts of a better future, and when she was disappointed time and time again, it hurt a little bit more each time.

Hope could be great, or it could be devastating. In her case, it had usually turned out badly.

"I've never particularly liked Seattle, but I have to say that this piece of paradise Joseph has managed to cut out for himself isn't too bad."

Misty jumped and then turned to find Bryson sauntering toward her. Dressed in a pair of dark jeans and a sweatshirt with a coat thrown over, and with a wool cap covering his hair, he looked younger and slightly less daunting than usual.

"Bryson. I wasn't expecting anyone to be up this early."

"I've always been a morning person. I took a jog about an hour ago and then went up to shower and change. I looked out the window and noticed you down here, so decided to join you."

"I haven't ever been to the beach to see a sunrise before," she said.

"The sunsets are a lot more spectacular than the sunrises on this side of the States, and the ocean is several miles to the west, but it's still nice to be out when the sky brightens. I'll have to take you to the East Coast sometime so you can see a proper sunrise."

She didn't want to ruin their moment and remind him that they weren't going to be seeing each other too much longer. And she had more of a chance of winning a lottery that she never bought tickets for than of standing beside the Atlantic Ocean and watching a sunrise with this man.

When his hand slipped down and took hers, Misty couldn't think of a single reason to pull back. His fingers felt warm against her skin, and she liked the idea of holding on to Bryson. If only she could hold on to him forever…

Maybe one of the reasons she was disappointed so often was because she dared to dream of things she couldn't possibly have. If she didn't set herself up for failure, then she would have no reason to be upset when things didn't work out the way she wanted them to.

But she could hardly think clearly and rationally when such

a handsome man was walking alongside her and holding her hand. Being here, around this family, around this man, was messing with her head. She needed to have this trial over with so she could settle into a normal life — whatever her new life, the new normal, was going to be.

Would she end up moving here? It made sense. She had no connections in Montana, nothing to hold her there. At least if she were here, she could find a decent job and get to know her family. Montana held nothing for her anymore — nothing but heartache.

"What will you do when this is all over with? Will you move?" Bryson asked.

How did he do that? He'd somehow read her mind again!

"I don't know yet. I received one of those community college catalogs in my mailbox a couple of weeks ago and was looking through it." Misty was almost embarrassed to say that aloud.

"That's great. What would you like to study?"

She glanced over at him, to see whether he was mocking her, or if he thought she was a fool even to consider such a thing, but he seemed genuinely curious. It gave her the courage to continue speaking.

"I honestly don't know. I was looking at the classes they offer, and there seemed to be some really fascinating subjects. I don't..." she paused, embarrassed to go on, but then she firmed her shoulders and decided to finish. "I...uh...don't have my high school degree, but I've always read a lot, spent hours in the library, and I found out that I can study for the GED through a community college, and the places I was looking at had easier admission requirements. I don't know how I'd even afford it, but it was just a thought."

"Where there's a will, there's always a way, Misty. I think that would be wonderful. And no matter where you decide to live, there are always colleges nearby. There are also a lot of online schools for those who can't get to a school, but I would suggest you go to a campus just so you can have that experience. Especially since you've missed out on so much already." As he spoke, his voice grew animated.

"I don't think it'll ever be a reality, Bryson. It was just something I was looking at."

"Don't do that." His changed manner, now stern and abrupt all of a sudden, stopped her in her tracks. He'd never used that tone before.

"Don't do what?"

"You are constantly saying what you can't or shouldn't do. Don't do that to yourself. It's not who you are. I see strength of will underneath the downbeat and downtrodden exterior you're trying to show the world. If you portray a weakling, then that's what the world will see. Do you want people to look through you? Do you want to fade away into nothingness?"

"I'm already there," she shouted. She was tired of listening to him lecture her.

"Only if you decide to be there. No one makes our destinies, Misty. No one! We can choose to let the world make us disappear, or we can stand up and shout back that we aren't going to take it. If you let yourself be kicked while you're down, then passersby will think that's acceptable and they will join in and start kicking you, too. Did you just roll over when you met me?"

"No. But I was frightened," she said, wrapping her arms around her now trembling body. It was cold and this fight seemed to be using up her energy, making her suddenly shiver.

"You've been frightened for most of your life and you've always fought back. Dammit, you should be one hell of a champion by now."

That wasn't something she'd thought about before. Was she a fighter? She'd gotten away from the foster parents who had abused her, escaped when street junkies had tried to do worse than abuse her, and she'd outsmarted a dirty cop. Maybe she was stronger than she gave herself credit for.

"Take my coat," Bryson said. He removed it and draped it around her shoulders, then pulled her close and wrapped her in a warm embrace.

"You'll get cold," she protested through chattering teeth. It was more emotional than physical, but she couldn't stop shivering.

"I'm made of solid steel. The elements can't hurt a superman like me," he replied, making her smile.

The wind was nipping at her neck, but she was warming up quickly as she stayed enfolded in Bryson's strong arms. This man was dangerous. He could uproot her entire life with a few words. He could make unspoken cravings rush to the surface.

But even knowing that, she didn't pull away; she just enjoyed the feel of his warm breath rushing across the top of her head as the wind stirred her hair. If she turned her face just a little, their mouths would align perfectly. The slightest tilt and those lips could be on hers.

She moved her head involuntarily, and then she was looking into his eyes, those warm gray eyes that hid so many secrets. And were able to draw her so quickly into their depths.

"Misty," he sighed before closing the minuscule gap between them and pressing his lips to hers. The cool air made their mouths tingle when they met. He pushed his tongue against her bottom lip, the softest of caresses. It was a question. Would she open to him?

Whether she wanted it to be or not, her answer had to be *yes*. She opened to him.

Bryson tugged her even closer as his mouth danced across hers, as he made her body ache with need. Tremors racked her body, and she snuggled tighter into his embrace, trying to satisfy a need that could be met only when the two of them lay skin to skin.

There was no hurry, though, nowhere to be but right there. He kissed the corner of her mouth, then her cheek, and her head fell back as his hot breath smoothed over the column of her throat.

He could take her now, right here on this beach, and it still wouldn't be enough. It would never be enough, no matter how many times their bodies joined, no matter how much pleasure he brought her. She finally understood the meaning of the word *insatiable*.

That's what she was — insatiable — at least when it came to Bryson.

In such a short amount of time, her life had begun to revolve around this man. It was a dangerous game, a game she was sure to lose, but for now, she couldn't make herself care.

His lips worked their way back up to her mouth, where he caressed her gently, kissing her bottom lip with such sweetness that she felt herself lift into a whole new plane.

This man was taking control over her every desire. She wanted to please him. And she wanted to be pleased by him.

Soon, the kiss went from sweet and gentle to hungry and passionate. Her core heated to dangerous levels, and her entire consciousness was fixated on having him strip her clothes away and sink deep inside her.

She grasped at his hair, holding him to her, while he explored her back with his hands, then let them move beneath the bundle of clothes she was wearing, and then climb up her sides until he was suddenly clasping one aching breast, the touch of his palm scorching her.

Before she could fall into an abyss of total pleasure, Bryson pulled back, his eyes almost savage as they gazed down at her, hot, hungry — ready.

"I want you every minute of every day," he said huskily.

"Then have me," she told him, too turned on to consider regretting her words.

The flash of need in his eyes, followed by a glance up the hill, made her feel like a seductress. With a boldness she would have never known she possessed, she moved her hands downward and squeezed the muscles of his tight buttocks.

"When we get alone..." he growled, then pulled back and enclosed her hand with his.

"Is that a promise or a threat?" she asked, feeling almost giddy.

"Both."

The way he said the word sent a shiver of anticipation down her spine. She'd made this big, strong man ache. She'd made him desire her — *need* her. She felt euphoric and found herself practically skipping as they made their way back up the trail to the house.

"I don't think I ever want to go back to the real world," she said with a sigh.

"I need this case to end," he replied, taking the glow right out of her. When she tensed, he halted their progress and turned to her. "So that I can be with you all I want — without the conflict of interest."

Her glow came flooding back.

Misty didn't believe their fling could last. But she didn't want to think about that. All she wanted to think about right now was the two of them lying in bed together, spectacularly sated.

"Why didn't you join me last night?" she asked. If he wanted her so badly, she didn't understand why he hadn't come to take what she was offering.

"Because Joseph would have somehow known and then strung me up as an example of what happens to men who defile the Anderson women," he said with a chuckle. "And, Misty, you *are* an Anderson."

"Maybe by blood, but I wasn't raised with them, and apparently my father was the black sheep of the family, so while they may be greeting me with open arms right now, that could all change in an instant. I've decided just to enjoy it while it lasts." She wasn't upset, just realistic.

"You will gain trust the more you get to know them. They're

the good kind of people to have in your life," Bryson assured her.

"I think you're right about that. But I don't think I'm exactly an asset to their superior blood," she said with a laugh, though her own words stung her.

"You are more of an asset than you could ever realize," Bryson said as they reached the back door.

"No more talk of this. I want to enjoy the next couple of days with this perfect family, and then, when I get back home — if you have time — I want to finish what we started down there on the beach." Misty sent him a flirtatious smile. Or at least what she hoped was a flirtatious smile. She'd hardly had a lot of experience handing those out.

"I'll move our flights up," he growled, cornering her on the porch.

"I wouldn't complain." She whimpered as his lips touched hers again and she melted against him.

"Well, I sure as hell would."

The two of them jumped apart quicker than a frog's tongue catching a fly as Joseph looked out at them from the doorway.

"We were just taking a walk," Bryson said, his cheeks slightly pink.

Misty was fascinated by his nervousness. Edginess from a man who seemed so confident all the time was fascinating to behold. But she could certainly understand it. Joseph was one heck of an intimidating man, especially standing in the entryway to his castle.

"Yeah, I'll just bet you were," Joseph grumbled, and he sent a warning look Bryson's way. Then a gleam appeared in the old man's eyes as he looked back and forth between the two of them. "Of course, a nice morning walk isn't such a bad thing."

Misty and Bryson gaped at him.

"Why don't we have breakfast and visit?" Joseph walked inside, absolutely certain the two of them would follow immediately.

And they did.

For the next few hours, Misty felt as if she were in an interrogation room. When Damien and Sierra joined them, she sighed in relief.

"Don't worry about Joseph. He just loves to be in charge," Sierra said as the two women escaped to a couch, leaving the men to chat among themselves. Soon, Katherine joined them, and Misty found herself really liking the soft-spoken woman.

The topic of Joseph and his wild schemes came up eventually. He thought he was being secretive, but it seemed that his antics were very well known.

"I can't figure out what Joseph's doing. He keeps talking about school, and marriage and kids, then he looks from Bryson to me. We're not a couple. We're just..." she trailed off, not knowing how to define their relationship.

"Yeah, I was just..." Sierra got a big smile on her face. "... just *nothing* with Damien, too," she finished with a giggle as she looked pointedly to the sleeping baby lying in her husband's arms as he talked with Joseph and Bryson.

Damien was so natural with his daughter, cradling her protectively in one arm while he rubbed along her soft bald head or patted her back gently with his free hand. He would look at her every few moments just to assure himself she was comfortable. *Awwwww*, Misty thought.

"Don't try to fight it, Misty. Just grab it while it's hot and then hold on for the ride," Sierra advised.

Though Misty blushed, she looked across the room at Bryson, and when their eyes met, a spark shot through her. Maybe her newly found sister-in-law was right — maybe she should just hold on and see where this all led.

She sent Bryson a wink. Would this work as a sexy gesture? Yesss! She felt immediate warmth when she saw him stiffen. Mmm, flirting was becoming a new favorite pastime of hers.

"You go, girl," Sierra said with a chuckle.

"I just might do that," Misty replied, leaning back and enjoying herself.

By the end of her second night at the Anderson mansion, she'd been talked into meeting the rest of the family. The Anderson Foundation was throwing a fundraising party and it sounded like too much fun to miss. Her last night there promised to be an adventure unlike anything she'd experienced before.

Bring it on, she thought with a new optimism.

CHAPTER TWENTY

"Y OU LOOK *STUNNING*," Sierra gasped after circling around Misty slowly so she could take in the entire effect of the gauze dress.

Misty clutched at the top of her gown and tugged, and Sierra jumped over and grabbed her hand. "Don't do that. You'll rip it and then be showing far more of your goodies than you are now," she said with a laugh.

"I *can't* wear this, Sierra. It's beautiful — the most beautiful gown I've ever even *seen*, because I certainly haven't ever *worn* one this stunning. But I *can't* wear this. Not in front of strangers." Misty turned back to the mirror in dismay.

Gazing back at her was a woman who certainly looked as if she belonged in this magical fantasy the Andersons had created, but it wasn't Misty. Her dark hair shone as it tumbled down her back, the bright sparkle of her green eyes was accented by expertly applied makeup, and her body...well, her body looked curvy and sensual, and...

"Nope. Can't do it," Misty sighed. "You have to have something more...more...I don't know, something that shows *less*?"

"It's a Cirque du Soleil theme," Sierra told her. "Just wait until you see what Joseph has planned!" She was practically bouncing on her feet as she held out a beautiful necklace and placed it around Misty's neck.

"Please tell me this isn't real." Misty brought her finger up and ran it over the large blue stone in the middle of a cluster of other brightly colored gems.

"Okay, it's not real." Sierra turned away to fasten her own jewelry around her neck and her wrists.

"What if I lose it?" Misty asked. This was getting to be too big of a deal. Maybe she shouldn't have agreed to go to the fundraiser.

"Don't worry; it's insured. Besides, if you lost it, someone would find it and take it to Joseph or Katherine," Sierra replied.

"Not everyone is that honest," Misty told her sadly.

"Anyone who comes here is. Now, come on, sweetheart. It's time to go." Sierra was not about to give Misty any chance to back out or change clothes, and she tugged the reluctant beauty from the room.

Then, Misty was slowly descending the tall, wide, polished staircase, and she could do little more than concentrate on not tripping in her silver heels. What sort of sickos were behind fashionable women's shoes? Seriously!

Stepping down the hallway — not quite gliding, but she was getting her stride on the mini-stilts — she heard music, and she couldn't help the pounding of her heart. This was like all the middle and high school dances rolled into one night. Except that she'd missed out on them all. No clothes, no dates. And she suspected that all the dances at the many schools she'd attended, even if you added them up and multiplied them by ten thousand, wouldn't have reached this level.

Got it in one!

When they entered through the silk-draped doorway into the massive ballroom, she stopped in her tracks.

It had been transformed into what looked like the sets of various Vegas shows. The ceiling had to be at least three stories high, it reached so far, and so many people were walking around, it seemed more like a real theater than a room in a home. Of course, Joseph and Katherine's home wasn't just a home. It was a castle that seemed to go on for miles in all directions.

Two performers were shooting fire from their mouths on one corner stage, while in another corner two women were performing an aerial "ballet" in silk that was draped from on high. Others were performing Cadre — acrobatics between two bars — leaping from one bar to the other, using only their legs in an amazing feat of strength. And one more stage featured several dancers moving in perfect synchronization, in what looked like a blend of a belly dance and hip-hop moves.

Misty was transfixed by the spectacles before her.

"Champagne?"

"Yes, please," said Sierra. She took two glasses and handed one over to Misty, who accepted it without looking. Her eyes were too busy. The ceiling was lined with glittering balls, light shooting from the crystals circling them, and the waitstaff were wearing brightly colored tuxes. The women wore the same jacket and top as the men, but sported skirts instead of trousers, and they all wore glittering half masks in different colors.

There was already a crowd, all dressed to the nines and exuberant.

I can do this, Misty told herself. Yes, her teal dress was strapless, and it dipped dangerously, its front held on only by ingeniously placed tape and who knew what else, and it had a slit clear up to the top of her thigh. Still, what she wore was almost modest compared with some of the other gowns in the room.

Since the costumes of the female acrobats were diminutive in the extreme, the men's eyes would surely be glued to them. She had nothing to worry about, she told herself.

After her second glass of champagne, Misty's worries diminished further.

"Ooh, I finally spotted Damien and Bryson," Sierra bubbled, and she took hold of Misty's arm and led her across the room.

"Sorry we're late, darling. We were talking with Lucas and couldn't slip away," Damien said as he leaned down and kissed his wife's lips. "You look good enough to ravish."

Though he whispered it, Misty heard, and her cheeks instantly flamed.

"Let's dance," said Bryson, gazing at Misty with pure heat.

She accepted his hand and followed him to the dance floor, where he pulled her against him.

"You are always beautiful, but right now..." he began and then cleared his throat. "Right now, it's taking all my restraint not to haul you upstairs and peel that dress away to see what it's barely hiding."

"We might get in trouble, Bryson, but I'm willing to risk it." She'd seen as much as she needed to of the circus acts. And there were so many people in the room, no one would miss them if they snuck away.

Bryson tensed as if thinking of an escape route. His eyes fixed on the door and he stopped dancing.

"I wouldn't try it. My dad will come looking for you," Lucas said as he stopped dancing next to them. "Hi, Magnolia. I'm glad to finally meet you. I'm Lucas, and this is my beautiful wife, Amy. I won't stand here and bother you all night, but we've tried to sneak out early during a number of dad's events, and he has a radar for potential escapees." He accompanied his warning with a laugh before he swirled his wife away, leaving Misty speechless.

"I think Damien told them not to hold you captive with conversation," Bryson said in explanation of Lucas and Amy's hasty retreat. "Your brother is worried you'll get overwhelmed by the throng of family members and you'll run off."

"I have to admit that that's how I've been feeling. There are just so many of them, and I don't know what to say, and I hate saying the same thing over and over again. It might be easier to just stand in a room with all of them and answer questions from a podium like the president does," she said with a champagne giggle.

"I could arrange that," he joked as they began dancing again.

"I'd kill you if you dared."

"You've already tried with your stun gun, and that ended up with you lying beneath me, so go ahead and try. I like the outcomes of our matches."

"I will best you, Bryson Winchester. Just you wait." She laughed as he spun her in a circle.

"I could dance with you all night, beautiful, but I'm parched. Let's get a drink, then come back for more."

After a couple of glasses of something blue — she had no clue what it was, but she loved the decorations on the large stick — boy, was she ready for the dance floor.

The hours whooshed by with dancing, meeting new people, and laughter. So much laughter. Who said clouds wandered lonely? As the Cirque acts continued, she was walking on them. Each member of the Anderson family she met was as kind as the last, all of them were easy-going and humorous, and they all seemed to be glad she was there.

She'd never be able to remember all the names. What she would remember was this fantasy world she'd been invited into. Joseph played a wonderful ringmaster, commanding his audience, and raising millions for his foundation.

The guests left with much lighter pockets, and they told Joseph it was by far the best such event they'd ever attended. At the end of the evening, hand in hand with Bryson, Misty found herself in front of Joseph and Katherine. Joseph's wife looked radiant in her golden gown.

"Thank you for inviting me to join you this weekend," Bryson said as he took Katherine's hand and kissed it, making her cheeks glow.

"It was a pleasure to have you, Bryson, and of course, to

spend time with you," she said as she kissed Misty's cheek.

"I hope to have you back *real* soon," Joseph said with a wink and a lift of his eyebrows as he looked to Misty.

"You are quite subtle, aren't you, Joseph?" Bryson said with a laugh.

"I'm too old for subtlety." He slapped Bryson on the back hard enough to jolt him a step forward.

Joseph kissed Misty's cheek, and she practically floated away to the sleeping quarters of the mansion, Bryson's hand clutched in hers.

"This night has been magical, Bryson. I don't want it to end. You have been the perfect companion," she said, leaning heavily on him as they neared the stairs.

"We all need magic in our lives. It keeps us young," he replied.

"I feel safe with you. Nothing bothers me, not the crowds, the noise, the cameras, the fear of Jesse finding me. It all goes away when we're together," she said, stopping to look at him.

"I hope you always feel that way. Sometimes," he paused and took a breath. "Sometimes, things aren't always black and white. Not everything can be placed in a box and neatly tied together with a pretty bow. Just know that, no matter what, I have your best interests in mind," he said. He hated to have secrets between them, and he was working up the courage to tell her about the DNA testing.

"I can't imagine feeling anything different. You are a hero in my eyes, and I have never trusted someone as much as I trust you," she said as they resumed walking and neared her door.

"I just hope that I'm worthy of your trust," Bryson said,

stopping and pulling her into his arms.

"Let's only worry about tonight for now." Misty looked meaningfully toward her door.

"I should kiss you goodnight. You've had too much to drink, and a gentleman would let you sleep it off," he said, his voice low and full of need.

"I'm not looking for a gentleman," she said, rising on her tiptoes and kissing the corner of his mouth. "I'm looking for a lover."

She was too tipsy to be shocked at her own behavior. And when he pulled her against him with a low growl issuing from his throat, and lifted her easily into his arms, she was glad to have pushed him to take her.

When the door swung open, she sighed in anticipation.

CHAPTER TWENTY-ONE

H E WAS NEARLY losing control. And he was still on his feet, walking. Yes, Misty was high in his arms. Her breathing was deep, and her dress was so low, he could almost — damn! not quite! — see her perfect nipples. How he wanted to taste them again, watch as they turned hard and wet.

But he wanted a lot more. He wanted to make her feel special. Because she was. She wasn't just another woman he would be enjoying beneath him. She was flinging open doors to emotions for him, doors that he hadn't known could be unlocked.

He was thinking of forever with this woman, and to lose that was unthinkable. He should hold off making love to her again and proclaim how he felt about her, but as he set her on her feet and she took a step back and reached behind her, he could do nothing but hold his breath.

This new, bold Misty was driving him almost to distraction. Tonight, she'd been transformed from the shy caterpillar to a beautiful butterfly. Not in looks — she'd always been beautiful, from the moment he'd first laid eyes on her with a Taser in her hand, no less. No, the transformation was in her confidence, in her self-esteem.

Bringing her back to Washington, making it possible for her to meet her family, to see the possibilities of where her life could go — that's what had made her blossom. She was no longer alone in the world. She'd no longer have to be afraid.

Bryson knew, beyond a shadow of a doubt, that with or without the Andersons, Misty was meant to shine. She had found her own way so far in life, and even with all the obstacles in her way, as he'd told her before by way of high praise, she'd managed to rise above the streets, with their attendant drugs, prostitution, and violence.

With the added benefit of her family — and not to brag, but him — there was nothing she wouldn't be able to achieve. He was grateful that he would be there to watch her break away from the shell she'd been in for so long.

But those thoughts inevitably gave way to other, more pressing matters, like the unzipping of the back of her dress. When her hands came back around, and she opened the sides…the dress still stayed in place. Bryson held his breath in anticipation.

"Tape," she said with a giggle, and she looked down at the fabric in front, which was hanging on just to torment him.

Unable to be out of her arms for a second more, he approached, commanding himself to take this slowly, to savor every taste, every gasp, every ripple of pleasure, and to make her fly so high that she wouldn't ever land again. Except, perhaps, on his bed, again and again and again.

"I will have to thank the designer of this dress personally," he murmured, then leaned down and kissed her...softly... slowly...with a tenderness that had her sighing in his mouth. He was determinedly taking from her all she was willing to give.

"Bryson," she moaned, before capturing his bottom lip with her teeth and sucking on it, sending jolts of electricity straight to his groin.

He could take her now and die a happy man.

When she ran her hands across his shoulders, slipped inside his jacket and tugged, he released his grip on her and let her send the garment to the floor. Better and better.

He felt her fingers flutter against his neck and loosen his tie before it floated to the ground. Then, one by one, she was undoing the buttons on his shirt, the sensation of her hands against his skin scorchingly sweet.

In his turn, he ran his hands along her exposed back, the silk of her skin hot to his touch — so satiny, so perfect in its imperfection. He reached the top of her buttocks, and his control almost abandoned him when he felt the minuscule piece of fabric covering that lush behind.

"You are so flawless, Misty, so unbelievably perfect," he groaned as she kissed his jaw, then sucked the skin of his neck before her mouth followed the course of her fingers and she kissed along the smooth planes of his chest, and the rigid muscles of his shaking abdomen.

She pulled his shirt free, then bit the skin of his stomach, nearly making him jump right out of his pants — and he certainly wouldn't have minded such a time-saver.

With calculated movements, she licked the skin of his stomach as her slim fingers began undoing first his belt, then the top button of his slacks. The sound of his zipper descending was oddly loud in the room, where the only other thing to be heard was their breathing, deep and desperate.

Reaching down, he gripped her head, holding himself steady as she slipped her hands under the waistband of his slacks and tugged. The material slipped easily from his hips and fell to the ground.

His erection stood out under the black underwear he wore, reaching for her touch. She shifted and kissed him through the silky material, making him groan as his legs fought to keep him upright.

No other woman had ever had this kind of control over him. And he loved it, loved feeling as if he were going to explode, loved knowing this was the last woman he would ever desire to touch…to sink inside…to pleasure.

When she rose back up his body, his stomach shook, his muscles tensed. He told himself to go slowly, to restrain his animal impulses. He was barely able to contain himself, but when she was standing and he found himself looking into her eyes, a calm fell over him.

Yes, his body was hard, yes, he was more than ready to complete their coupling, but, also yes, he could be happy just to hold her close the entire night — the rest of his life.

"You make me…feel. I'm falling in love with you, Misty," he whispered. He bent forward and kissed her, keeping his eyes open to look into her mystified gaze.

"We don't know each other well enough," she said, confusion and hope fighting for supremacy within her fragile psyche.

"I know all I need to know, Misty. I know you love with all your heart, though you're afraid others won't love you the same way. I know you like to make little doodles on paper when you are sitting somewhere and bored. I know you can't keep still, that you have to move. I know you like sappy movies and sappier books, though you try to hide your obsession. Yes, I've looked at your shelves. I know that you are the most beautiful, caring, strong woman I've ever met. And I also know that I can't go a single hour without thinking of you, and when I tried to stay away from you, I could barely function. I want to be with you — not just tonight, but forever."

Hope was the winning emotion in her eyes.

"I think about you all the time, too, Bryson," she admitted. She kissed his jaw, her body trembling in his arms. It wasn't quite an undying confession of love, but from her, it was a lot, and he appreciated her words.

"Then why should we fight this?"

"I can't think when you touch me," she said, sighing when he kissed her neck, then trailed his tongue along her shoulder.

"Then don't think. Just feel." His hands slipped inside her dress and he pulled it slowly away from her breasts, letting the fabric float to the floor, leaving her standing before him in nothing but a scrap of lacy black fabric covering her core.

"Oh…" he said in a long rush of breath.

She smiled at the passion in his gaze, confidence now shining in her eyes as she spun in a circle in front of him, letting him get a good view of her rounded derrière, then facing him and showing him the perfection of her breasts, her nipples peaked with desire.

Unable to keep himself from touching her, he brought his hands to her hips, slid them over the curve of her behind, slipping his fingers under the soft material at her hip, moving higher, covering her stomach, and then caressing her breasts, his palms rubbing across her hard nipples, making her gasp, making her entire body shake.

He walked her backward until her legs made contact with the bed, and she fell; she lay sprawled out before him, her hair gloriously mussed, her eyes shining, and her chest heaving, her body begging for his mouth to claim every inch of her skin.

He ran his mouth along the smoothness of her legs, spending extra time on the delicate skin of her toned thighs, and then he skimmed across her womanhood, encouraged by the moans escaping her throat, loving the way her body arched to reach for his mouth.

His hands roamed where his tongue wasn't, and he touched and kissed every inch of her, leaving his mark on her thighs, stomach, chest, and neck, and making her mouth swollen from his kisses.

She writhed beneath him, begging for him to complete their union, begging for release — and he gave it to her. He returned his complete attention to her heat and helped her fly over and over again, leaving them both exhausted as he continued stroking her flesh, tasting her, loving her.

When he moved up her body, he took her breasts fully in his hands, weighed them, squeezed them, then sucked her nipples deep into his mouth, nearly giving her another orgasm.

"Please, I want you inside me," she begged, her head twisting back and forth on the mattress, her skin covered in a light sheen of sweat, her eyes half open, a remarkable light shining from them.

Removing the last barrier between them, he quickly took care of protection, and then spread her legs wide as he pressed against her core. Inhaling deeply, he took a moment just to appreciate the beauty of her beneath him.

"Now, Bryson," she commanded, in her need for him, now sure both of herself and confident he would comply.

"Like this?" he teased, slipping an inch inside her. This game was killing him, but having her struggle beneath him made his misery worth it.

"No!" she shouted, her short nails digging into the skin of his hips as she tugged on his body.

"Mmm, like this?" he asked, pushing another couple of inches inside her, before pulling back out.

"I swear…" As she began to threaten, he thrust fully inside and buried himself deep, taking their breath away at the perfect fit.

"You were made just for me," he groaned. He pulled back again before quickly sheathing himself in her heat once more.

"Yes…yes…yes," she moaned, gripping his skin so tightly that he was sure to be black and blue.

He didn't care.

Minutes or hours passed. He didn't know. All he knew was that each time he pulled from her, he was empty, and each time he sank back into her folds, he was complete. A glorious pressure built, limbs and mouths entwined, and somewhere along the way, they became one, one breath, one heart beating, one body, reaching for paradise.

When they peaked together, both moaning out their pleasure, she opened her eyes, and he gazed into them, knowing this was it — this was their moment. Their fates were sealed, and he would never let her go. With a guttural cry, he exploded, his body shaking from the intensity of his release, while her body clung to him tightly as it pulsed around him.

With barely enough energy left to move, Bryson still managed to pull her into his arms and stroke the slick skin of her back as the two of them floated back down to earth, reveling in what had just occurred.

Bryson was no fool. He knew this moment was beyond anything he'd ever experienced before. He knew when he had everything he could ever dream of.

As he fell asleep that night with her in his arms, he knew that the rest of his life was going to be right.

He just didn't know that there might be a few bumps along the road.

CHAPTER TWENTY-TWO

S HE'D ASSUMED SHE'D be relieved to head back home, away from her brother and everyone else in the house. What if they knew exactly what she'd been doing under their impressive roof?

They probably did; she couldn't miss their knowing looks. Thankfully, no one had called her on it. She would have been mortified. So when it came time to leave for the airport, it was *almost* a relief — *almost* being the key word.

No, saying goodbye wasn't as easy as Misty had thought it would be.

She couldn't repress a few tears as she and Bryson pulled away; the sight of Joseph and Katherine, Damien, and Sierra with the baby all standing on the step waving made her heart ache in a way she hadn't experienced before.

For right now, they appeared to have embraced her as one of their own. If they still felt that way when the newness wore off, she'd be more than happy to be a part of their family.

Family. That was something she'd never thought she'd have — and she certainly wasn't going to throw it away.

Soon the case would be over, and Jesse would be locked behind bars. She had to tell herself that. And then she'd grow more confident about the future. Then, her real life could begin.

For now, she had Bryson at her side. He was there to keep her safe. He was there to make sure this man who had terrorized her for so long never got the chance to do it again.

But she had a bigger fear than Jesse. Was she confusing love with something else? Bryson had been the one to show up and tell her Jesse wouldn't be able to hurt her again; he'd been the one to show her how wonderful life could really be. He'd taken her to the edges of paradise and beyond and then slowly floated back down to earth with her.

But did all that mean that she was falling in love with him, or was she actually just grateful to him? She hadn't ever fallen in love before and had no idea what true love felt like. She knew what her heart felt, knew that the thought of being with him for the rest of her life sounded just about perfect, but she didn't know if she could trust what she was feeling.

Maybe the best way to judge the way she felt was if she were away from him for a while, even a few days. She'd been in this whirlwind relationship — if *relationship* was the right word — and she hadn't had time to pause, hadn't had a chance to really think.

She'd gone straight from one situation to the next, each one new, each one a first in her life, and more exciting than the next. There had been fear, passion, excitement, and sadness.

All of these emotions sent her whirling. She needed to land on solid ground again before she could properly assess what she felt beneath all the adrenaline.

At the airport, Misty knew she was being unusually quiet, but there was so much on her mind. She wanted to speak to Bryson about it, share her feelings, but she certainly didn't want to do it in public.

He'd shared with her the night before, so she didn't think the conversation was going to go badly. It was more that she was afraid of how she felt, not of how he felt. Still, he could be riding on the same emotions as she was, and also be confusing love with something else.

Didn't men confuse love and sex?

Hadn't she read magazines before that said if a woman wanted to keep her man, she needed to feed him well and give him great sex — something about being a lady during the day and a tramp during the night?

Ahhh, she couldn't remember. But if she could make him confuse the two things, would it be to her advantage? Or would everything crash and burn?

The time passed quickly, and soon they were boarding the plane. Misty sat back in the comfortable first-class seat, and decided she'd drink a screwdriver. A bit of alcohol couldn't hurt, though it wasn't yet 5 p.m. Yeah, yeah, it *was* somewhere.

She was trying to work up the courage to talk to him about these serious matters when the two of them weren't naked or about to get naked. There was no chance of that happening while they were in flight, not unless she wanted to become a member of the mile-high club. And, no, she did not.

The plane took off, and soon Bryson turned to her with a worried look in his eyes that didn't reassure her.

"I have something I really should have told you sooner, but…I just didn't know how to say it," he began.

"You can tell me anything, Bryson," she said, though her heart pounded.

"It's really not that big a deal…"

"If it's not that big a deal, why are you having such a difficult time saying whatever it is that you need to?"

"Okay, here goes…" He took a long drink of his diet soda before continuing. "Joseph didn't tell you how he found you, did he?"

Misty was silent as she processed his words. This wasn't what she'd been expecting. What did Joseph have to do with their feelings toward each other?

"Um, no. I guess that should have been the first thing I asked. I was just in too much shock over the whole situation."

"Well, I've known Damien for quite some time. We've never been particularly close friends, but we see each other a few times a year. I knew he was looking for a sister. I also knew she would be about your age."

"Just tell me, Bryson. I don't know what that has to do with anything." So far, he hadn't cleared anything up.

"I took a glass from your house, had your DNA compared with Damien's." This time, the words rushed from his mouth before he lifted his glass again and drained the contents.

"May I get you another drink, sir?" The flight attendant approached and Misty wanted to shout at her to go away.

"Yes, please," he replied, and Misty waited while the woman

took his glass, then brought him a fresh drink.

The more she thought about what he'd done, the more irritated she became. Why couldn't he have just spoken to her about it? Told her his suspicions, said that he might know where her brother was? Why had he been so underhanded?

"Isn't that illegal?" she asked instead.

"No. Well, stealing your glass is theft, but not testing your DNA. Once you discard something with your DNA on it, it's fair game in most states," he said.

"So, should I press charges for theft?" She was only half kidding.

"I supplied them for you," he reminded her, and that just pissed her off more.

"So you set me all up, and that means you get to do what you want?"

"I know I should have told you what I was doing, but try to understand. I was doing what I thought best to protect you. I didn't want your hopes to be raised if it turned out that he wasn't your brother." He ran a hand through his hair in frustration.

"Great. That's what I need, Bryson. I need you to keep babying me. You told me you were falling in love with me, but how can you love me if I am this weak little girl who needs you to hold my hand at every moment of every day? This visit has finally given me some confidence, made me see that there's so much I can do. What you did has knocked me back down a step, saying you're the big, tough guy — the heroic FBI agent — who will just take care of everything for me. How is that caring about me? How is that protecting me?" she whispered furiously, not wanting the other passengers to overhear them but starting not to care.

"I'm not trying to hold you back. If I could attach the wings to your back to help you fly, I would. I just wanted to take care of you, and I still do. Is that so wrong?" he demanded, his own temper flaring.

"Yeah, Jesse just wanted to control me, too. That's really what this is about, isn't it? You are the man and I'm the meek little woman, so I need to just bow down and be grateful when you do something for me that *you've decided* is in my best interests?"

"I'm done with this conversation, Misty. It all turned out well. I can't believe you would even compare me to that man. He is a worthless piece of trash," he said, fury flashing in his eyes.

"Well, I'm done, too. I need to think about this, Bryson." Misty didn't like it at all that he was now telling her when a conversation was going to end.

As the plane started its final descent into San Francisco, Misty wanted to break the awkward silence between the two of them, but she couldn't seem to find the right words. She knew she was being unfair. Yes, the way he'd obtained her DNA was wrong. Yes, he should have trusted her more with the truth, but hadn't she been a frightened woman when he'd found her? Hadn't she trembled in his arms?

She knew he'd done what he had with good intentions, even if he had gone about it all wrong. She just didn't know how to call a truce.

They had time.

Then the plane ride was over and done with before she could come to any conclusions, and they were silently walking side by side as they left the terminal. Just when she was working up the courage to apologize, or at least to try to work this fight out, his phone rang.

When he snarled into the device, they both stopped, and she turned his way anxiously.

"Why in the hell not?" he thundered. His voice was normally more controlled, but between their fight and whatever was happening on the other end of the line, his mood appeared to be growing worse by the second.

There was a long pause as the person on the other end of the call made some little speech or other, but whatever he or she was saying wasn't making Bryson happy. Misty waited quietly for him to continue speaking.

"Fine. I will be there, but heads are going to roll…" Another pause. "I said, *I will be there*. Send a unit to check Misty's house." Yet another pause. "No, not the damn marshals; they'll be around later anyway. I want our guys."

Misty waited while he stopped and looked up at the sky in exasperation.

"Good. Jackson is on his way? Okay. I'll be there in a couple of hours."

Bryson hung up, his face now blank as he took a long breath. "I'm sorry, Misty, but I have another client — he's just a kid, been really messed up. I can't say anything about the case, but he ran off yesterday and they're just now bothering to call me. Jackson, is going to make sure your house is secure. I should be back within a few hours."

"Don't apologize for doing your job, Bryson. I think that's the thing I respect about you most — how committed you are to your work. We will talk later," she said, shifting on her feet. She couldn't tell from his expression whether their talk later was going to be good or bad. Maybe he was finished with the drama of being with a woman like her.

"I love my job, but right now isn't the best time to leave," he said, looking away from her as he focused on what he needed to do. She shrank inside just a little bit more. Was he thinking of the kid he needed to help, or was he pulling away from her?

Usually, a fight meant the relationship was over, at least in her world. It was either over or she was about to get the hell beat out of her. She knew Bryson would never hurt her physically, but she'd almost rather suffer through that than go through the heartache of losing him. But she was going to stay strong right now.

"You have to go. I'll be fine," she told him.

"I could drop you off first," he said, but from the anxious look on his face, she gathered that the boy had run off in the opposite direction.

"I've managed to survive, even in some sticky situations, for a very long time. I assure you that I can get home." She turned toward the line of cabs.

"Here's cab fare," he said, stepping up after her.

"I've got it, Bryson. I do have a job," she reminded him, her back stiffening.

"I know, but you're not making much," he said, holding the money out to her.

"Believe it or not, it's enough to survive."

"Are you sure you don't want me to take you?"

"Go right now, or I'm going to take back what I said about respecting you for being so dedicated to your job."

After a final look her way, a look that she couldn't interpret, he turned and jogged off, toward where his SUV was parked. Misty watched him vanish into a sea of people, and she scoffed at herself when she felt a surge of anxiety.

What they had was going to go one of two ways. It was either over — or it would truly begin. There was nothing she could do about it at the moment, so she needed to focus on what she *could* do. Right now, that was to get home. She had to work that night, so she would get only a few hours' sleep, if she could sleep at all. Then, hopefully tomorrow, she and Bryson would talk.

If the uneasiness in her chest would go away, she'd feel on top of the world after her visit with her brother, or at least as high as the Empire State Building. The fight with Bryson shouldn't have affected her so much, not after the wonderful days she'd had in Seattle.

The line for a taxi moved quickly, and soon she was on her way home. The sun dipped in the sky as she pulled up to her house.

Home, sweet home — for now, at least. Misty paid the cab driver and stepped wearily from the car.

It had been a lovely trip, but she was tired straight through her bones. Having a panic attack and then meeting her family had been overwhelming. Add to that not sleeping much because of certain nighttime activities, and the math was clear: not enough sleep. To end the trip with a fight, and she was done for.

Stepping up to her door, she unlocked it and carried her bag in. "Nap time!" she said to the dark entryway as she dropped her bag and dragged herself down the hallway.

When she stumbled over something, it took her a moment to realize it was a body. *What? Who?*

It was too late by the time she knew she wasn't alone, realized her skin was crawling, her heart was shouting to her to run. It was too late, because a hand holding a cloth came up and covered her mouth and nose, and then all she saw were dots before she lost consciousness.

CHAPTER TWENTY-THREE

B RYSON WAS DRAINED and ready to drop. Finding Ricky had been a lot more difficult than he'd thought, and the kid had been about to make a huge mistake with the lighter and the torch that he had on him. Yes, the kid wanted to get the gang who'd killed his mother, but he was only going to end up joining her in the ground if he didn't let the law handle it instead of waging a futile vendetta of his own.

She wouldn't have wanted that for him. She'd loved her son and had taken him out of the embattled neighborhood they'd been living in so he wouldn't grow up to be in a gang or to deal drugs. The people she'd left behind hadn't been happy about her escape, and they'd found her. It was just one more nail in that gang's coffin, since they were under surveillance for narcotics, murder, and various other major crimes.

They would pay — Ricky just had to give the lawyers and Bryson time to do things the right way. After a lot of talking, Ricky had backed down and was now securely back at the safe house, where those worthless bastards couldn't touch him.

Bryson stopped at a gas station and stuck the nozzle into his tank, then went inside for coffee. After paying for his drink, he walked back outside and checked his messages. He was concerned to note several missed calls from Axel. He hadn't heard the phone ring. Maybe he'd been too focused on Ricky.

He quickly dialed Axel's number.

"Winchester, where in the hell have you been?" Axel yelled from the other end of the line.

"I've been with Ricky. I'm tired, cranky and in need of a whole lot of sleep. Quit the yelling," Bryson said as he took the nozzle from the tank and slipped into the driver's seat.

"He got away from surveillance!" Axel shouted, his voice higher than normal.

Bryson's muscles locked together and a cold sweat popped out on his brow. He didn't want to ask the next question.

"Who?"

His voice was so quiet, he wasn't sure whether Axel had heard him. After starting his motor, he had to sit there for a moment and wipe his palms on his trousers.

"Jesse Marcus."

Bryson couldn't get sound through his throat, couldn't focus. He sat there for a moment, took a deep breath and tried to be rational. Jesse was in Montana — Misty in California. Even if the asshole had gotten away, he couldn't reach Misty. Jesse could have no idea where she was.

"She's safe. Her house was checked before she went home tonight," he said, trying not to panic. He was at least an hour from her place.

"She's not home, Bryson. The marshals have been by her place. There's no sign of her, nothing. And no one has seen Jesse since yesterday. He's had plenty of time to make it down there."

"But the house was checked," Bryson repeated. He'd made sure.

"They found the agent...dead," Axel said.

The breath rushed from Bryson's lungs. Jesse might have her — he might have taken her anywhere. But how could he have found her? The records of her location were sealed.

"He can't know where she is!" Bryson shouted, more scared than he thought he could ever possibly be.

"It doesn't look good," Axel told him. "This guy...he has connections, Bryson. I don't know how or who, but I do know he gets his hands on information he has no business knowing. He gets away with stuff he never should have been able to get away with. As you well know, even this trial has had problems since the start, with evidence turning up missing, witnesses that should be protected ending up dead. I don't know who's helping him, but someone is, someone with a lot of power."

Yes, Bryson knew this — knew all of this, yet he'd still allowed her to go home alone. He'd been confident in the fact that Jesse was being watched, that they'd be warned if the man appeared to be getting even an inkling of where she was. He'd promised to protect her, sworn she wouldn't get hurt.

What if leaving her at the airport cost him Misty forever? What if she thought he didn't care?

"Do we have any clues on where he could be?" Bryson asked as he threw his SUV into drive and peeled out of the gas station, hitting the freeway and flooring the gas pedal.

"I'm working on it, Bryson," Axel said, but he didn't sound confident.

"I don't care what you have to do, but get me something," Bryson shouted into the phone. Maybe they'd missed a clue at her house, something to tell him where Misty could be. He had to find her — had to save her, because he knew beyond a doubt that Jesse had her.

Bryson's world had been too perfect for it to continue without a glitch. Misty might never trust him ever again if Jesse hurt her. He'd broken his promise that he wouldn't let Jesse near her.

"I'll see what I can do," Axel said.

Bryson wanted to slam his phone through the windshield. "That's not good enough, Axel. I don't want you sitting on your ass thinking up ideas. I want you to find her!"

"I know you're scared, Bryson, and I know I'm the one delivering the news, but don't talk to me that way. We're going to get her back." Confidence and steel now ran through Axel's voice.

They were both pissed — for their own reasons. Bryson tried to calm down, but he couldn't. There was too much left up in the air. He felt vulnerable, helpless.

He slammed the phone down on his seat, nearly smashing it. Not wise. If she could call him, he needed to be available. He only hoped he wasn't speeding away from her as he rushed toward her house.

No matter where he had to go, or what he had to do, he *would* find her before this night was over, he vowed as he raced down the freeway. One way or another, she was coming home — even if Jesse ended up in a body bag. To think she could be in one too wasn't acceptable, and he thrust that grim thought from his mind.

Turning his emotions off, he prepared to do whatever it took to find Misty. Because he would die before letting her go.

CHAPTER TWENTY-FOUR

SOME GUY WITH a jackhammer was hard at work inside Misty's head. *What the heck?* It took her several moments to orient herself and to remember.

She'd paid the cab driver, walked into her house...

Panic set in when she recalled the body on the floor. And then someone had grabbed her, drugged her. Where was she now? The room was dark, with only minimal light sneaking in beneath the door. Was she alone?

As she sat up slowly on the putrid-smelling bed, her hand landed in something sticky and wet. She shook as she yanked the hand away and wiped whatever it was off onto another section of the uncovered mattress. Her stomach heaved and she tried to plug her nose. Hearing a scratching in the wall, she felt herself freeze.

Was that rats or mice? Fear was threatening to consume her, especially since the lighting was so poor. Where was she? It seemed to be an abandoned building of some sort, somewhere now inhabited by rodents and bugs. As if her situation weren't bad enough, she had to fight vermin, too. Not that she wasn't dealing with a human form of vermin…

Forcing herself not to succumb to panic, and not to shed futile tears, she attempted to look around, and to make her breathing calm down. Creeping quietly over to the window, she looked out, but she couldn't see anything through the dirt-encrusted panes.

Don't freak out, she reminded herself. Easier said than done. She had no idea where she was — but she had a pretty good idea of who'd brought her there.

Her fears had come to life, just when she'd started to feel more secure. She'd been so afraid that exactly this might happen, and now it was real, now she had to fight to survive. And she had to do it alone.

Did Bryson even know? Or, more like it, would he care? After their stupid, petty fight, maybe he wouldn't bother to check on her. Okay, she knew he was a professional, and he wouldn't let his probable disgust with her petulance stop him from attempting a rescue, but how would he even know where to look?

When would he check on her again to even learn she was missing? It might take several days before he tried to find her. Why had she had to get so upset with him? Yes, he'd been wrong in surreptitiously having her DNA tested, but it wasn't worth this. It wasn't worth her now being all alone with Jesse in what had to be the middle of nowhere.

It seemed hopeless. So freaking hopeless. But *NO*. She *would not* cave in to her fears. She couldn't!

What she needed to focus on was escape. She attempted to open the window, but to no avail. It was nailed shut, or glued shut, or it just hadn't been used in so long that it was never going to open again without a crowbar.

Taking a deep breath, she thought about her options. She refused to just roll over. She'd never, ever been a quitter. She'd grown up in the most awful of circumstances, and she'd managed to survive this long on her own. She would continue relying on herself — the one person who hadn't failed her.

Her phone!

Please be there, she screamed in her still-pounding head, and she reached inside her bra and found the small device. Her years on the street had taught her lessons that she still carried with her now, and one of those lessons was not to leave something you didn't want to lose in obvious places.

Holding her breath now as she stared at the door, she pulled out her phone and flipped it open. One bar of reception, and only a single bar of battery life. It was enough…she hoped.

She didn't even think about calling 911. Instead, she dialed the one person she truly did trust, no matter what had been said — Bryson. When the phone began ringing, she heard the doorknob rattle on her room, and she fought down the stomach-roiling nausea. Now was not the time to vomit.

Quickly turning the incoming voice volume of the phone way down, she hid the device inside a hole she'd found in the pillow on the small cot, she prayed it wouldn't disconnect, prayed Jesse wouldn't hear it, and prayed even harder that Bryson would be able to trace the call. Then she moved to the other side of the door and waited for it to creak open.

If she could get the jump on him, she would have half a chance.

There was no other plan than that. She knew she wasn't going to just lie on the bed and wait for him to rape her...and then take her life when he was done playing.

"Miiissstttyyy," Jesse called in a singsong voice as the door opened fully and light spilled into the room. It took a couple of seconds for her eyes to adjust to the new brightness. "What the hell?" he snarled as he stepped inside, moving toward the bed.

It was now or never.

Moving with a speed born of desperation, Misty slid out the door and ran for her life.

"Get back here," he bellowed, whirling around and following her in close pursuit.

She made it to the living room. Yes, they were in a house, one that looked as if it was either condemned or needed to be. Grime covered every surface and the furnishings were sparse. From there she dashed to the kitchen, where she turned in a circle so she could try to get her bearings, and found herself looking into the cold, calculating eyes of her former abuser.

There was no door in this room. She'd made a wrong turn. *Don't panic. There has to be a door. You just didn't see it.*

"I've been waiting for you to wake up. I thought about climbing on and taking a ride with you knocked out, but that wouldn't be any fun, would it? I want to hear you scream. You know how it turns me on." Jesse spat on the floor as he sauntered into the room, looking as if he had all the time in the world for his little cat-and-mouse game.

Though her heart was nearly exploding inside her chest,

and the blood felt frozen in her veins, she tried to hold it together. She absolutely could not show weakness or it would cost her something more important than just her life — it would cost everything she'd worked so hard to build since she'd escaped him.

Looking over this Goliath as he took another step closer, she saw a chink in his armor. The last year-plus hadn't been good to him. He was about twenty pounds heavier, the weight all in his stomach, sweat was rolling down his brow, and he was breathing heavily.

"It looks like you've been partaking in a few too many of the free doughnuts at your weekly cop meetings, Jesse." She was proud that her voice came out confident, snide and demeaning.

His eyes widened before they narrowed.

"And it seems you've grown some false security in your time away from me, little girl. Don't forget that I managed to get the jump on you once tonight. I will have you screaming beneath me in just a few minutes." His face lit up at the prospect.

"Yeah, you're a real big man, aren't you? You managed to sneak up behind me and use chloroform. I see you were too chicken to just face me." She wanted to look for an escape route but was too fearful of taking her eyes off the despicable SOB.

He was still huge, especially with the added weight, but he didn't look as intimidating as she remembered him. At least he wasn't in his cop uniform, so there wasn't a gun sitting on his hip. It would almost be better to have him just shoot her, though. She'd much rather have that happen than feel his sweating body thrash on top of her.

Never. She'd never allow this man inside her again. He wouldn't touch her — she'd kill him first.

"Oh, I'm a big man, all right, Misty. I'm the man who will teach you some respect," he said, the sweat now pouring out in his anger.

Maybe it wasn't the wisest move to piss him off, Misty realized, but if he was talking, then he wasn't formulating a plan on how to get her.

"Yeah, a real man who can only go after women." Damn. Her fear came through in her voice that time.

"I should have tied you down. I thought it would be more fun to do it when you were awake…while you were struggling. That's always turned me on, sweet little Misty."

His gloating made her stomach heave. How had she managed to put up with his abuse for so long? It would have been better to be one of his murder victims. At least then she wouldn't have to deal with his stench.

As they faced off, he moved forward again, his intent clear — to box her in. She edged away successfully. If she could figure out how to get out of this house, she knew she'd have no trouble outrunning him. She had a reason to live now. Two reasons. A family. And a man she loved. A man she would apologize to profusely if she could just see his face again.

"I'm going to play with you all night. For days, actually, taste your body…over and over again. It's going to be so good. You won't be recognizable when I'm done with you, but that won't matter, because you won't ever be found. I imagine it will take me a while to grow tired of your sugar, though, honey buns."

"You won't touch me again, Jesse. Never again."

"We both know I will. If you give up this chase, I'll make the first time a little less painful," he said, light shooting from his eyes in anticipation.

"If you back off, I won't kill you," she replied.

He lunged for her, and she quickly sidestepped him, then rushed to the next room as he went flying to the floor with a scream of rage. *Pissed was good*, she told herself. The more angry he was, the more careless. If she could just tire him out, she could get out of the house.

"You are only making this worse for yourself, Misty. Stop this now, before I really lose my temper."

Jesse had trapped her in the next room. She'd made another foolish move. There was a door, but it was boarded up, without offering her even a chance of getting out of the house.

She looked around quickly for any sign of a weapon. Nothing that she could spot.

Dammit!

"You won't touch me, you disgusting maggot," she growled, and she scooted around the ripped couch.

"Oh, I'll be touching you all night long," he replied, his beady eyes glowing with desire as he drew closer.

"I'd rather die, Jesse."

"Don't worry, dollface, you will," he promised. "But not before I get what's owed to me."

There! A knife! She spotted it in the corner of the room, on the other side of the couch, beneath what looked like an old television stand, and its blade was at least six inches long. Though it was rusty and old, it could probably do some damage. If she could just get her hands on that, she would thrust first, ask questions later. Though she'd threatened to kill him, she really didn't want to live with that, with knowing she'd taken another person's life. But she sure as heck wanted to maim him, to do anything short of killing to stop him.

And if it came down to her or him, well…

When he jumped toward her this time, she was prepared. She leapt over the coffee table and rolled onto the ground, crawling closer to the broken stand. Almost there!

When her fingers were within grasping distance, pain shot through her ankle as he grabbed it and twisted. He had hold of her from beneath the coffee table, his body lying on the ground, a trickle of blood running down his head from some hit he must have taken during their struggles. She only wished she'd seen the impact.

The wound must have been slowing him down, but not enough, and if he applied more pressure, her ankle was going to snap.

"Give it up, bitch!" he thundered as he managed to get his other hand on her leg, and he began pulling her back toward him.

"No!" she screamed, clawing against the floor. When she thought it was hopeless, she managed to grip some of the torn carpet, anchoring herself before she tugged, though she felt as if she were being ripped in two.

"Now you're mine," he said, and laughed.

Her heart stalled as her blood turned to ice, but still, she wasn't giving up. He might outweigh her, he might be stronger, and he might have the upper hand, but she had a reason to live, she reminded herself.

"I love your spirit, Misty. Always have. You fight so much more than any of the others. Even after days of my beating you, you managed to glare, managed to cry out in anger as well as pain. Most of the girls submit far too quickly, take all the fun away. Not you, though. No. You've always thought you were tough, and you never did fully submit to me. I like that in a woman — like the spark. It will be a shame to slit your throat. I don't know if I'll ever find another one like you. Don't worry, though, I won't kill you too fast. I want to enjoy that lush little body for as long as I can."

He clearly thought he'd already won, and his sadistic arrogance filled her with rage.

"I fought because having your revolting body on top of mine is a fate worse than death," she spat, tugging as hard as she could on the leg of the TV stand to gain traction, the muscles in her arms screaming, the bone in her ankle screaming, too. It was worth it, however, because she managed to pull herself forward the two inches she needed to reach her goal.

He was so focused on her legs, on trying to pull her back to him as he yanked at her clothing, that he didn't see her fingers slip around the handle of the knife.

She knew she'd have only one shot at this, only one chance to plunge the blade into his thick flesh. If she messed this up, he would win. And that was something she absolutely couldn't let happen.

"I don't give a damn what you feel about me, just as long as you scream when I get my pleasure," he growled.

Maybe she shouldn't have been taunting him, because his rage was reaching new levels, but it *was* distracting him, and she needed that.

Her pants ripped under the intensity of his grip. The sound excited him, and he pulled harder, drawing her backward, now fully within his grasp.

He scrambled up her body, and slammed his fist against the side of her head, making her see stars. Jesse had one hell of a punch; he'd knocked her out more than once in the past. It took everything in her not to black out right then. If that happened, she'd lose all chance of escape.

So, okay, one chance, she told herself, and when he flipped her over onto her back and hovered over her, spittle dripping from his mouth and landing on her chest, she thrust the knife upward and twisted, not aiming, no strategy in mind except to wound him, to push him away.

"What the fu –?"

His sentence ended in a pained grunt when the blade sank deep into his stomach, and he began to collapse on her. With the last remaining ounce of strength left in her, Misty shoved against him, and he rolled onto his side, giving her just enough room to drag herself away.

He screamed as he twisted and flopped over onto his back, then reached down and pulled the blade free, making blood spew from the wound.

Misty thought it was all over for her. She had only wounded him, not stopped him. Now he was probably going to carve her up and then do unimaginable things to her as she lay there dying, unable to fight back.

Tears sprang to her eyes when she leapt to her feet, but she ignored the pain in her left ankle as she stumbled from the living room and searched for the front door. There had to be a way out.

Jesse started to rise, then collapsed to the floor, groaning, while blood oozed from the deep wound. Maybe she'd done enough; maybe she'd make it out of this hell.

"You'll pay…" he cried, but he fell again as he tried to get to his feet.

It was now or never. If she didn't get out of this house, he was going to do whatever it took to kill her. This wasn't a game to him anymore. This wasn't about violating her body. This was now revenge because she'd managed to hurt him — and no woman was allowed to hurt Jesse, not to his way of thinking.

Limping down a hall, she finally found the door to the outside, freed the locks, and managed to wrench it open despite the blackness threatening to overpower her.

"Help, please," she called out, trying to scream just in case anyone was within hearing distance, but her voice came out as little more than a squeak. Stumbling off the rickety porch, she made it only about twenty feet from the house before she fell to the ground.

She should have gone back for her phone, but it was too late now. There was no way she'd go back inside. Her frustration mounted as she moved away from the porch light and the eerie darkness swallowed her.

She — and Jesse — were indeed in the middle of nowhere. Crawling on her hands and knees, she found a woodshed and struggled around it, then collapsed.

Her will to live was great — but the pain was unbearable. Her only hope was that Jesse wouldn't get back up, and that her call had gone through. Bryson would be her last thought before unconsciousness pulled her under.

She wondered what it would be like if, despite everything, the two of them could live happily ever after, if they could forget about the case, about the fight, about everything but each other.

If Jesse got back to his feet and found her, she'd never know...

CHAPTER TWENTY-FIVE

B RYSON'S PHONE RANG and he glanced down, then felt his heart stop momentarily. He hit the button and was about to shout into the microphone. That's when he heard Jesse's voice in the background, a voice that would haunt him the rest of his life. He'd spent hour upon hour watching the scumbag on video surveillance, and in the interrogation room when they'd brought him in, and he knew that ugly voice intimately.

Though he'd already known that the bastard had her, it hadn't fully sunk in until the sound of that man's voice came through the phone. He knew better than to say anything, knew she'd most likely hidden the phone, *knew* he mustn't give away the fact that she had a phone on her, but it still took everything inside him not to shout, not to order Jesse to leave her alone.

Hitting mute so that no sound would transmit through her line, he tore into a gas station, nearly wiping out the fuel dock in his hurry. Leaving the SUV running, he dashed inside.

"Give me your phone now!" he shouted to the terrified young man attending the register.

"I'm not allowed to," he stuttered.

"I don't have time for this," Bryson snapped. He leapt over the counter, pushed the kid aside, and reached below the counter, dialing the number he had memorized.

"I need a cell phone tracked right now," Bryson said as soon as the call was picked up.

"Yes, sir." It took only minutes, but those precious minutes felt like hours. Once he had the address, he called in every favor he had owing to him.

"Get them there now!"

With that, he hung up and rushed from the store. Entering the address on his navigation system seemed to take forever, and he realized his fingers were shaking.

Bryson paused and took a breath, then held out his hand. Okay, he was calm. She would take care of herself and he would get there in time.

He was about twenty minutes away according to his navigation system. Slamming the gearshift into drive, he tore out of the gas station and rushed through traffic, pulling around speeding cars as if they were standing still.

His mind whirled as he whipped around corners, and he took the turn onto the gravel road at nearly seventy miles an hour, sending the SUV into a spin. Not smart. Working with the gas and wheel, he managed to straighten the vehicle out, but he let up a little on the gas. He couldn't get to her if he crashed, and if he blocked the road with an overturned vehicle, the other responders wouldn't get to her either.

Feeling as if he were crawling, he made his way down the winding road, five miles to go, three, two, one... When he was a quarter mile away, he pulled off the gravel and cut the engine, unwilling to give Jesse any warning that he was there.

He moved swiftly through the dark night, his flashlight guiding him, and he didn't hesitate as he approached the abandoned hillside house. A light shone from the porch, and he saw the door open and Jesse stumble out, a blood-soaked shirt covering his upper half.

He hadn't spotted Bryson, who was just outside the glow that the porch light was casting.

"Where are you, bitch? I'm going to slit you from your neck to your..." Jesse started coughing and couldn't complete his threat, but Bryson had no doubt what the slug had intended to say.

Jesse tripped over his own feet, and flew off the porch, and then Bryson heard a groan at the same time Jesse did. It came from behind the shed. Jesse turned his head, and Bryson, watching the scene unfold before him, stepped from the shadows as Jesse held up a gun and staggered to his feet.

"Stop now, or I'll shoot," Bryson called out. He'd never wanted to just fire his weapon so badly, but he knew he had to give a warning, or he was just as bad as the scum he'd be firing upon.

Jesse turned slowly in Bryson's direction, and was close enough now that Bryson could see the wild look in the man's eyes. Instead of dropping the gun, Jesse pointed it. With no hesitation, Bryson aimed and fired.

Jesse screamed and fell back flat on the ground, his kneecap shattered. Unbelievably, his hand rose and he attempted to catch Bryson in the gun's sight.

Bryson aimed again, and this time the bullet putting a hole straight through Jesse's hand, and his gun flew ten feet away. The man started whimpering and sobbing. "Please don't kill me. I give up. I give up!"

Bryson stepped over to his gun first, kicking it farther away from Jesse, then he approached the man cautiously, not taking it for granted that Jesse didn't have another weapon on him.

"You have the right to remain silent…" Bryson began, while twisting the man's arms behind his back and cuffing him. "I would love it if you just did us all a favor and bled out right here," he added in a voice of deadly calm at the end of his recital of Miranda Rights. Then he searched his clothes and found another gun in the back of his pants. Bryson tossed it toward the other gun after emptying the chamber.

"You have to get me help. That little bitch stabbed me," Jesse whimpered as snot ran from his nose.

"Yeah, you tell all your buddies how that petite woman got the drop on you, Jesse. You know, they really *love* cops in prison. They like to make you *their* little bitch. You won't have to worry about rough sex anymore, 'cause you're going to get plenty of it."

That swine would never lay a finger on Misty again. Walking carefully over to the shed, Bryson announced his approach. "It's me, Misty — Bryson," he called out as he circled around the dark building, pulling out his flashlight and shining it on the ground.

When he found her in a heap against the outside wall of the

shed, he rushed to her side, terror almost making his muscles seize up. "Misty?" he called softly, dropping to his knees and feeling for a pulse. It was strong. Her eyes fluttered as he checked for injuries. When she didn't complain as he touched her neck and back, he carefully lifted her onto his lap. "I'm right here, baby. I'm so sorry I let him get to you. I broke my promise," he told her, his throat choking with emotion.

"Bryson?"

"Yes, it's me. Help is on the way."

"I knew you'd come." Her eyes opened and she looked up at him with relief.

He could barely see her from the glow of the flashlight lying next to them, but what he could make out sent a whole new level of fury through him. He wanted to march back over to Jesse and beat him until he wasn't breathing.

He lifted his hand and gently caressed her face, tracing around the smooth skin on her temple where a nasty purple bruise was forming.

"I'm sorry for getting mad, Bryson."

"Aw, no, baby. You were right to get mad. I was wrong. But none of that matters right now. All that I care about is getting help for you. With this little stunt, Jesse won't be able to worm his way out of trouble. You won't have to hide ever again," he promised, leaning down and kissing her forehead.

"Thank you, Bryson. I've been so scared, but I'm okay. I beat him. I got away." A couple of tears of relief drifted down her cheeks.

"You are so strong, baby, so very strong," he said. "I knew you could do it. You're a fighter — and you don't give up."

"I didn't give up. I just…my head hurts so much, and I think my ankle is hurt pretty badly." She moved to snuggle closer to his warmth.

"I should have been here sooner, Misty."

"No. I'm glad…" She had to take a deep breath. "I'm glad I did it. I beat him. I'm not going to be afraid anymore," she said, and she gave him a weak smile.

"That's right. You have always amazed me," he told her, and he ran his fingers through her hair.

"I'm really cold, Bryson."

Damn. He felt like a complete jerk for not thinking of that. Careful not to jostle her, he removed his coat and draped it over her shoulders as he heard sirens screaming down the drive.

"Help is here. I'm going to stand up and bring us out into the light so we don't spook them," he said.

He rose carefully, keeping her cradled against him, and he was walking toward the front porch as the first cop car screeched to a halt a few feet from Jesse's trembling body.

"I'm the one who phoned you. My name is Special Agent Bryson Winchester," Bryson called out when the officer jumped from his cruiser with his gun drawn.

"Walk slowly, sir," the police officer said, "and don't make any sudden moves."

Bryson walked to the car. "My badge is inside my coat pocket, on Misty here."

The officer took the coat carefully and found the badge. "Thanks for your patience, sir. Is this Jesse Marcus?" he asked, indicating the man lying on the ground and groaning.

"Yes. He's been stabbed in the abdomen, and shot in the kneecap and hand," Bryson said just as the ambulance pulled up.

The paramedics rushed out and Bryson took Misty to them. One attended to her, while two more rushed over and looked at Jesse.

"He'll live," the paramedic said, and he rolled his eyes just a bit.

"Good. I want him to have a nice long stay in prison," Bryson said. Jesse would get what was coming to him.

"Oh, I can almost promise that," another officer said. The police took it as a personal affront when one of their own went bad and gave everyone with a badge a bad name.

Soon, while Misty was being patched up, Bryson was able to run back and get his SUV. Then he transported her to the hospital, where she could have a full workup. Her ankle was severely sprained, and she'd have to wear a soft cast for a while, but at least it wasn't broken. Jesse must have really put some pressure on the delicate bone.

Bryson so wished he'd gotten at least one punch in. It was too late now. The bad cop was already squealing faster than they could write down the information he was providing — giving them names of people the FBI never would have thought to suspect, and bringing down everyone he could with him in an attempt to reduce his sentence.

It wouldn't help him, but it would certainly make the streets of Montana a much safer place to be. And, not to their surprise, the conspiracy went well beyond their state, all the way to Washington, D.C., and included some very surprising players.

By the time Bryson was able to take Misty home in the early hours of dawn, he was exhausted, but feeling so good about her safety that he didn't care a bit.

"I can walk; I may just take a while," she said with a laugh as he carried her inside, her foot nice and secure in its cast.

"I like carrying you," he said, and he bent down so she could unlock the doors.

"I like you carrying me, too," she said before kissing his jaw. "I won't be staying in this house anymore, will I?"

"Nope. Jesse will remain locked up now, and his trial will start real soon, unless he agrees to a deal, which it looks like he's doing. We can now take you back to Montana," he said as he made his way to her bedroom.

He thought she'd be relieved to go back to her real name, and to leave this episode in her life behind her, but disappointment flooded her features.

"I've never lived in a place this nice," she admitted as he laid her down.

Ah, that was the problem. "I know of a beautiful four-bedroom home that overlooks the lake and has deer who are unafraid to come and take an apple right from your hand."

"Oh, that sounds beautiful, but something like that would be priced far too high for me. Plus, it would probably be wiser for me to be close to town so I can get a good job while I go to school."

"It's only about a ten-minute drive to town, Misty, and the roads stay plowed in the winter. It only gets bad when a freak storm hits."

"Still…"

"The price is right, too. It would only take one piece of paper and you could own the place," he said, unbelievably nervous as he lay down next to her and looked into her eyes.

"What? I'm confused," she said as she reached up and ran her fingers through his short hair.

"Marry me, Misty. Come home with me and live in the mountains of Montana. Let's fill our log cabin with a dozen pets, and hopefully a few two-legged creatures as well."

Her eyes grew big, and he couldn't believe how frightened he was that she might turn him down. His heart was in his throat.

"Are you sure, Bryson? I mean, maybe it's just the adrenaline from the situation, or maybe you think you love me and you don't, or maybe —"

"I love you, Misty, more than I could ever show you. Yes, our relationship has been intense, but that's not why I love you. I love you because I can't go a single day without thinking of you, and when I thought I could lose you, my world stopped having any meaning. I love you because you make me want to be a better person. I love you because you're you." The truth of his words shone brightly in his eyes.

She was silent for a minute, and his heart thudded as he waited on her verdict.

"I love you, too, Bryson, so much more than I thought I was capable of loving anyone. I want all of that and more." Tears of elation welled up in her eyes and a bright smile flashed across her face.

Bryson pulled her into his arms and held her close,

knowing that his future was now set. There wasn't anything they couldn't accomplish as long as the two of them were together. He planned on a lot of beautiful tomorrows.

EPILOGUE

I CAN TELL he's going to have my rugged good looks."

Misty laughed at her brother as he held her newborn son in his arms. "Yes, Damien, he certainly has his uncle's eyes, or at least it appears that way right now. It's a bit hard to tell with them closed all the time."

"Don't you be taking credit for all the hard work I put into my son," Bryson said. He looked down at the baby, his pride evident.

"What hard work? It wasn't like that part wasn't enjoyable," Damien said with a laugh.

"Hey, who do you think had to drive into Taco Bell at two in the morning every time she wanted her favorite Crunchwrap Supreme?" Bryson asked.

"Yeah, I kind of miss those late-night-craving runs. Sierra was so adorable when she was pregnant," Damien said, a fond smile on his face. "Of course, I gained a few pounds from all the junk food." He patted his perfectly flat stomach.

"Well, it's a good thing you like me pregnant, because…" Sierra said.

Everyone was silent as they turned toward Sierra, who was glowing in happiness.

"Really?" Damien gasped.

Bryson took his son from Damien's arms before his brother-in-law could drop the baby in his excitement. Damien rushed over to Sierra and lifted her into the air, hugging her gently before kissing her with a passion that looked as if it would never die down.

"Really," she assured him with a big smile.

"Oh, that's wonderful," Misty said, and she held out her arms for her son. Bryson put the child right where she needed him to be.

"What are you naming the young lad?" Sierra asked when Damien finally stopped kissing her.

Misty looked at Bryson, who nodded. They'd discussed names and both had a favorite. "Paxton Damien Winchester," she said, and then noticed a suspicious sheen in Damien's eyes before he turned away and coughed.

"Oh, that's beautiful," Sierra said.

"Yes. Paxton was my late grandfather's name, and, well, obviously, you know where Damien came from," Bryson said, his own eyes bright.

"That's a fine name," Damien said when he turned back around, no hint of tears anymore.

"I thought so," Misty told him. "My life has turned around so much since meeting you and finally getting to have a family. My only regret is that I didn't know you my entire life." She had enough tears for all of them.

Damien moved over to the bed. "Oh, Misty, I have the same regret, but we can't go backward, so we just have to fill our tomorrows with as much joy as we possibly can." He leaned down and kissed her on the forehead.

"Yes, I agree," she said.

Misty had never imagined that her life could be blessed with so much joy. She was married to Bryson, and she was falling in love with him a little bit more every day. She now had a beautiful son, one whom she would cherish and whom she hoped eventually to give some sisters and brothers. And she was finished with her first two semesters of college. She hadn't picked a major yet, but she had plenty of time for that. Right now, she was just enjoying moving forward — not standing still and definitely not falling back.

Someday she would be like the rest of the Andersons. She would be able to build her own place in the business world, and even be a tycoon. Yes, she liked that thought — she was a tycoon in the making.

"I love you, wife," Bryson said, and he kissed her gently before rubbing his son's little bald head.

"And I love you, husband," she replied.

She had decided that fairy tales and magic had to be real. She'd gotten a little bit of both the day she'd met and Tased Bryson Winchester.

The End

If you would like to be notified when Melody Anne releases a new book, go to http://www.melodyanne.com, and sign up for the email list.

page intentionally left blank

page intentionally left blank

27798073R00160

Made in the USA
San Bernardino, CA
17 December 2015